JUST ONE YES

JUST ONE YES

NICHOLAS COURSEL

FIRST EDITION.

Edited by Bodie Dykstra.

Cover by Alejandro Baigorri.

ISBN: 979-8-9853571-0-3

Published by South Lake Books, 2022.

to R,
with love

Sensory overload came from every direction. Principal Jennings tried her best to cut through the noise and give us all a worthwhile conclusion to the last four years, but the roaring crowd drowned her out. None of us cared. High school was almost over.

We were graduating.

Eager moms snapped pictures of their beloved graduates-to-be while their husbands and the rest of the family laughed and wolf-whistled, shouting incoherent names across the packed gymnasium. It'd been a slow boil. Four years hard-time, finally served in full. We were all ready for it to be finished, for the euphoric release of the real world to come crashing down in the form of whatever came next.

A barrel-chested dad stood from his seat with his hat turned backward. He cupped his hands around his lips and yelled something unintelligible over the hardwood, but nobody heard it. The surrounding cheers were far too loud. I looked down the stage and smiled at my best friend Finley as Principal Jennings cut her conclusory speech short and gave us all the signal.

Our tassels moved from right to left and we stood up from our seats. The end of the road stood under our feet; caps thrown in the air to continued applause. I took a step forward. Everyone around did the same, and we walked to the end of the stage together, fundamentally changed from the way we'd walked on.

We had graduated.

Standing near the edge of the stage, I looked across the hardwood for a sign of my mom. I scanned the bleachers up and down until I found her in the middle of the third row, cheering. We made eye contact, but it broke quickly as Uncle Andrew grabbed her shoulders and pulled her into a constricting hug.

I shook my head and walked off the stage in a single file line with all of my newly former classmates. We trudged forward toward the converging mob of parents. Then, suddenly, a familiar voice cut caught my attention, "This isn't working. I think we need a break from each other."

Turning around, I found myself staring into my girlfriend's eyes. They were big and blue and beautiful, eyes that I had looked forward to seeing every day for over three years.

"What did you just say?" I asked through tight lips, praying that I'd heard her wrong.

"We need a break," she repeated, speaking with a sense of finality the second time around. "This isn't going to work."

I couldn't believe what I was hearing. My hands shook as I looked at her. "What do you mean by that?" I questioned. "Why won't we work?"

"We're going to college soon," she explained, sighing into the bottlenecking crowd of parents and freshly minted graduates forming around us. "Everything's about to change, and if we stay together, I'm scared we'll end up hating each other."

Several families began stepping forward. The walls were closing in. They were all so desperate to see and hug and take pictures with their freshly graduated babies that they hardly noticed us. They had absolutely no idea what was going on. Our lives were inconsequential.

"Come on, Tory," I said, knowing full well I was practically begging. But I didn't care. I needed her. I needed us. "We've been together three years. You can't throw that away on the off chance that we *might* end up hating each other one day."

"It's for the best," she mumbled. "We need this, both of us. You can't see it now, but you will—trust me."

I took a step back and wiped a sweaty hand across my forehead. It was cold and clammy, trembling. Exactly how I felt.

"I'm sorry. But this is the only way."

Shaking, I took a step back, nearly vomiting all over the hardwood. There was nothing I craved more than Tory's touch, for her to tell me it was all a lie. But I knew she wouldn't. She was out of reach. We were gone, and my insides were folding inward. I took a second step back, then turned away, avoiding her eyes.

Mom and Uncle Andrew were walking toward us, laughing and smiling. Uncle Andrew held a camera against his left eye. The other was half-closed, squinting into the view finder. He'd stop walking every few steps, hold his breath, and press down on the shutter button to snap a picture of me and Tory. This process repeated itself until they'd reached us.

I forced a smile and waved at them. Tory pivoted and did the same. "Please don't hate me," she whispered into my ear before disappearing into the crowd.

Her void was quickly replaced by Mom and Uncle Andrew's exuberant presence. They were the last people I wanted to see, both radiating with a sense of pride I didn't dare break by telling them what had just happened. If I did, they would overcompensate horribly, and it would make everything so much worse.

So I put on a fake facade and acted like everyone around me, like I was happy. Uncle Andrew pressed the shutter button on his camera down one last time while Mom pulled me into a hug. There was a blinding flash of light; a moment forever preserved.

"Look who it is," said Uncle Andrew in a slow, deliberate drawl. Shivers went down my spine as I looked into his big green eyes. "Our little graduate. How's it feel to finally be done?"

"Congratulations," Mom said, ruffling my hair. She refused to let go. "We're all so proud of you. You did it, you really did it. You finished high school. You're a graduate!"

I didn't say anything, just continued to smile. All I wanted was for Tory to come back, but her back kept moving further away and I knew that she wasn't. Maybe she never would.

When she reached her friends on the other side of the gymnasium, they welcomed her gleefully into their circle. They laughed and posed and took pictures that would populate their Instagram feeds for weeks to come. She fit right in, like nothing had even happened.

Uncle Andrew grabbed me by the shoulders and threw an arm around my neck. "You should be smiling right now," he said, pulling me loose from Mom. "Cheer up. You're finally free."

She pulled me into another hug seconds after Uncle Andrew let me go again. She asked him to take a few pictures of us, and he happily obliged, snapping away until she laughed and shook her head and said that I must be tired of all the pictures and constant onslaught of attention. Naturally, I lied, so the cycle continued. They switched positions and took twenty or thirty more.

"Do you mind if I go catch up with Tory?" I asked once Uncle Andrew put his camera away. "She's right over there, with her friends. There's something I forgot to tell her."

"Of course I don't," Mom replied. Her face looked happy, but I could tell from the creases under her eyes that she was disappointed. "Get over there. Today's all about you guys."

"Meet you at the party?"

She nodded. I hugged them both one more time, then they turned away and walked out of the gym side-by-side. And I was left alone, utterly helpless eyeing Tory from the wrong side of the gym. She was still huddled with her group of friends laughing and taking pictures.

That all stopped when we locked eyes; her smile fell. I pushed myself through the crowd while they all openly stared in my direction. She whispered something to them before I stepped into earshot and they all walked away. The gymnasium was full, but finally, we were alone.

"Don't make this harder than it already is," she said before I had the chance to plead my case. "I've made my decision."

"But we're perfect for—"

"No, we're not. This is what we need."

"How could you be so heartless?" I asked, voice quivering. "Is this really how I get treated after spending three years together?"

Her eyes darted to the people behind me as I spoke, scanning the room left to right. "It's for the best," she whispered.

People were beginning to congregate around us, snickering and whispering amongst themselves. I had no idea what they were saying, but knew it couldn't be good.

"You don't want to do this," she continued. Her eyes were intense and stared into mine without blinking. "Not here, not right now. This isn't what you want. Trust me, Louie."

"Just tell me what I did wrong," I begged. "That's all I'm asking for. Give me a straight answer and I'll leave right now. I'll go my way and you'll go yours. Come on. It's the least I deserve."

"You didn't do anything wrong," she replied. "It's just that I'm going to school in England and you're going to school in Chicago. Everybody knows long distance never works."

"You make it sound so clinical."

"Staying together just doesn't make any sense."

"Love usually doesn't."

"Staying together will only prolong the inevitable. It'll only make things worse in the end."

"Who says there has to be an end?"

"There's always an end."

"Maybe you're right," I conceded. "But can it really be worse than this? What pain are we saving here?"

Tory took off her cap. Its tassel dangled limply over the side like a worn-out flag of concession, lifeless. She sighed, defeated, and stared down at the floor. "I've made my decision."

"So that's it?" I asked. "We're through, just like that?"

My pain lingered thick in the air, nearly palpable. I looked up from the hardwood and met her gaze. Her eyes were cold, glossed over, almost. There was nothing left for me to say.

We were over.

Blinking away a wave of unsolicited tears, I turned away from her and faced the growing crowd. "What're you all staring at?" I asked, palms facing the sky. "Don't you have anything better to do? Pictures to take, parties to go to, something—*anything!*"

A few of them left, but most remained. They pulled their phones out in response to my outburst, holding them high as their cackling swelled to a roar. Tory tucked her head down and slipped away, disappearing into their ranks. Once again, I was all alone in a packed gymnasium.

Three years had been boiled down into a fifteen-foot walk across the hardwood of our relationship. The entire school laughed from the deepest pits of their bellies, recording Snapchat videos that would forever immortalize my worst day. I tried walking a-way, but it was no use. Their laughter was inescapable. The tears began to fall. Nobody loved me. None of them cared.

A familiar voice spoke into my ear, and an equally familiar arm wrapped around my neck, "Are you okay?"

I turned and saw Finley staring into my tear-stained eyes. His long, curly hair protruded out in every direction beneath his cap. A weak smile rolled over his face. "Not at all," I replied.

"What's going on?" he asked. "I saw you talking to Tory, then she left and everybody started laughing."

"We broke up," I said simply. Each word was a dog fight with my upper lip, a fight I was unsure that I could win. "We broke up. And no, I don't want to talk about it."

"Right. Okay. That makes sense. Don't worry about what happened. Let's just get out of here. I've got something in my car that will make you feel better."

I had no idea what he was talking about, so I remained apa-thetic and shrugged. Whatever he had waiting, I didn't care. It didn't matter. The day couldn't get any worse.

My eyes fell to the floor, lingering there. Four dress shoes were all I saw before the black, then the gravity of the moment truly hit. I would walk out of the gymnasium's doors never to return again.

It was all over, everything—high school.

The ice-cold metal from the door ripped me out of my cascading thoughts. I opened my eyes to a kaleidoscope of shaky grays and blues convalescing in the strangest, most erratic of ways. In my desperation to escape their laughter, I'd walked directly into the graduation banner. It was all over me.

A loud rip accompanied my next step forward, followed by a feverish blur of crinkling paper constricting tighter and tighter around my body with every movement. The laughter swelled; my breath cut short. Sweat tumbled from my brow, staining the tops of my shoes along with the hardwood. I flailed my arms around in a desperate struggle for freedom, but the paper kept constricting. I couldn't get loose.

Flashes of blinding white light cut through the thin paper as I continued to flail. They were all taking pictures of me, and their laughter confirmed it. My stomach burned, cheeks red. Tears began to form around the edges of my eyes. They fell hard.

"Stop," said Finley's voice, firm as it cut through my paper chamber. "Stop moving—*stop!*"

I resisted at first, arms swinging, but Finley grabbed me by my shoulders and held me firm. "Relax," he mumbled under his breath, then ripped me free. "Are you okay?"

"What do you think?" I snarled, kicking pieces of the banner from my shoes. *Go Tigers*, it once read. *Congratulations Class of '16.*

My cheeks were blood red. They continued to laugh.

"Forget about them," Finley, leading me forward. We stepped into the hallway together. Thankfully, it was mostly empty. The vast majority of the school was still back in the gym, laughing hysterically. "Forget about them. They don't matter."

"But she does. She does, and she always will."

Finley shook his head, but said nothing.

2

The highway was bustling as we merged, speeding away from our newly former high school. Cars cut in and out of our lane. Lifted trucks honked impatient horns, then bustled over the exit ramps leading all across America.

I gripped the hem of my pants anxiously. For some reason, Finley reveled in the chaos. Weaving through the lanes of traffic, he passed three separate cars in quick succession. A few of them honked, but that only encouraged him. Whenever there was a close call and we almost hit someone, he would just glance over at me and smirk, then go faster.

"Where are we going?" I asked as we crossed seventy. "The party's all the way on the other side of town."

"I know. We have to make a pit stop first."

I groaned, "Where?"

"The park. It'll be quick."

Stopping at the park was the last thing I wanted to do, but Finley was a man on a mission, obsessed, and I didn't have the minerals to put up a fight. So I just sighed and stared out the window. "Let's hurry and get this over with."

"No way," he replied. "I've got a surprise for you. Something to take the edge off. You desperately need it."

The fresh pavement of the highway quickly became cracked and dilapidated as we approached the park. I sighed again and shook my head, but didn't say anything. Finley pulled onto an overgrown patch of wild grass and weeds behind the old baseball field, then shifted his car into park. Neither of us got out.

"This is the perfect spot," he explained, reaching over me to dig into the glovebox. He got elbow deep before pulling back out and gesturing toward the space behind us. "Those trees block the wind perfectly. Keeps the blunt lit."

"Who cares about the wind?" I asked. "Hurry up. I want to get out of here. I'm ready for this all to be over."

He grunted in response, dismissing me in favor of continuing his search. "Here we go," he muttered finally, pulling a small gray box from the glovebox. He held it up for a moment, then tossed it onto my lap. "This should make you forget all about Tory."

I opened the box. A small Ziplock baggie was folded neatly inside. My nostrils flared, insulted by the pungent smell. I took another breath and examined the scent in closer detail. It was distinct, incredibly so. Despite having never tried the stuff myself, I knew exactly what it was—marijuana.

Throughout four years of high school, Finley must have asked me a thousand times if I wanted to smoke with him, but I always said no because of Tory. She lamented constantly about how it would ruin his life, and mine too if I ever tried the stuff. It would keep me out of any college worth attending, but she was gone and her opinion didn't matter anymore. "Light it up. Why not?"

Finley smiled and pulled a small, tightly rolled blunt from the baggie. He brought it slowly to his lips and let it rest there. It dangled right on the edge, yet never quite fell off. A cherry red Bic came from his front pocket. He held it up, clicked—the blunt burned a sudden orange. His eyes ignited the summer.

"To freedom," he said, exhaling as smoke escaped from either side of his mouth. "And college, never looking back."

After taking another puff for himself, he passed me the blunt. I took it from him gingerly, handling it with the care you'd assign any foreign object you'd yet to make an appraisal of.

The blunt felt so out of place in my hand, so uneven and awkward. I put it between my lips like Finley had and held it there a while. Orange grew deeper; smoke overwhelmed me. I took a breath inward and let it fill my lungs. They burned. It was less smoky than I'd been expecting, yet twice as rough. There was a palpable edge to it, too. Before I could go for another hit I broke out into a terrible fit of coughing and passed it back.

Take two hits, then pass. The rotation worked back and forth, interrupted only by my constant coughing. The more I inhaled, the more acutely aware I became of my body and all the strange things it did. Every movement I made, every breath that I took. It was all wrong and abnormal.

My thoughts tumbled and fell into a cold basin filled to the brim with paranoia. No wonder Tory wanted nothing to do with me. Who would? I was a pathetic excuse of a man. That's what my brain told me, speaking as loudly as it could. Our breakup had always been coming.

She deserved so much better, so much more.

• • •

Finley's marijuana had fully kicked in by the time we arrived at my party. I felt like a stranger in my own skin. My eyes tingled back to front. Everyone was looking at me. They were all staring, hanging onto every word I said, preying.

They all hated me. Of course they did, I knew that much for sure. Each step I took forward confirmed my suspicion; a new set of judgmental eyes burning into my soul. And they all wanted to talk. Usually a quick "congratulations" or "have fun at school" sufficed, but some of them wanted more, a full conversation coupled by my undivided attention, both of which I couldn't—and also refused—to provide.

So I continued walking, giggling to myself. "Do you think they know?" I whispered to Finley.

"Know about what?" he retorted. One of my cousins reached

out and shoved a stuffed white envelope into my closed fist. "The weed, or what happened with Tory?"

Just as she had begun to slip from my mind, he'd said her name and she was back, even worse than before. Her face and all its beautifully wretched features were burned into the backs of my eyelids. "Both," I grumbled.

"They probably know about what happened with her already, but definitely not about the weed. We're good. We drove the whole way here with the windows down. There's no way we smell."

The tingling sensation behind my eyes grew stronger. It was almost overwhelming. "Even if they haven't yet, they will eventually," I replied, glancing around. "I wasn't good enough, so she left me. That's what they'll say."

Finley wrapped an arm around me and pulled me into his chest. "It's time for bigger and better things. Think about all the girls at Northwestern."

"They won't be her."

"She won't cross your mind after a week."

"You're wrong. I'll never forget her."

"This is your last go at Long Beach, take it before the big city sucks you in and refuses to let go. Don't waste your time thinking about Tory and what could have maybe happened one day."

Before I could respond, Uncle Andrew slipped through the crowd, exclaiming my name at the top of his lungs. He jostled past Finley and stood directly between us. "I must've missed you coming in," he yelled over the music. "How are you feeling? Must be sad to see it end."

"Something like that."

He laughed from the pit of his stomach before bringing me into yet another hug, a hug so tight that it constricted my left arm and pressed it tight against his waist. I itched my eyes with my free hand and tried pushing him off, but failed miserably. He just squeezed me tighter and tapped his calloused fingers into my back, making time like a perfect metronome. His chest heaved softly: up and down, up and down, up and down. The tingling continued.

"Enjoy the freedom while it lasts," he went on. "You've got four more years before the real world hits you."

"Yeah, yeah," I muttered.

I could see Mom over his shoulder, so I fought hard and finally managed to wrestle free. I nearly ran over to her once I had. She was working diligently on the cake, cutting it into small slices as a group of my younger cousins watched. They all held plates in their hands, waiting, inching closer and closer.

"How's the party going?" she asked. "Do you like it? Was it too much? Are you having fun?"

"It's perfect," I replied, forcing a convincingly eager smile onto my face. "Thank you—for everything."

"Try the cake," she encouraged. "It's red velvet with vanilla frosting, your favorite. Take a bite and let me know how it tastes."

I dipped my index finger into the frosting, let it linger there a while, then licked it off. It was creamy, white, and felt surprisingly cool against my tongue. I closed my eyes and rode the tingles all the way down. Pure bliss. Oh, had I been missing out.

"That face tells me everything I need to know."

"It's amazing," I said. "Perfect, everything is. You were right all along. I'm glad you forced me into this."

Her smile grew. I found myself being wrapped into another hug. It was much softer than Uncle Andrew's had been, more delicate and a lot nicer too. My chest fell; my eyes shut. The tingling grew, tickling from behind. I collapsed into Mom's arms, smiling, and momentarily forgot about Tory and graduation and everything else. I was a child again, nothing more.

Then she let me go. "Pretty good turnout," she said. "Nearly everybody showed."

I glanced around. She was right. The outdoor pavilion was filled with people celebrating me and the great life I was about to embark on. But without Tory, I struggled to see the point.

"Isn't it wonderful?" she asked.

"Perfect," I replied absentmindedly, silently asking myself why any of it mattered. Without her, none of it did. "I should probably be mingling right now."

"I guess everything can't be cake and fried chicken."

"Wouldn't that be nice?" I turned around.

"Make sure you talk to everybody!" she yelled after me, shouting into my back. "And don't forget to say thank you!"

Finley held a clean fork in his hand when I reached his table. Uncle Andrew had just left and he looked grateful for it. His plate was heaping with double portions of uneaten ham, gravy, and mashed potatoes. All I got was a quick nod when I sat down, then the shoveling began.

"I can't believe she'd do that to me," I muttered maniacally into the tablecloth, speaking to no one in particular. "After all these years, everything we've been through. I just can't believe it."

"Forget about her," he said again. Small pieces of ham fell from his mouth with every syllable. "All you can do is move on. It's the only way forward."

"But look at all this." I gestured violently toward all the people and decorations surrounding us. "It all reminds me of *her*. High school this, graduation that. No matter what I do, I can't get away. There's no escape."

Finley stood up and glanced around. "You're right. So let's get out of here. How's the beach sound?"

"Yeah," I scoffed. "I wish."

"Half the town's already there."

"But what about the party?" My gesturing continued, more intense the second time around. "All these people are here for me. I can't get up and leave. Mom would kill me."

"She just wants to see you happy."

"Maybe so, but she won't like it."

"Come on," Finley urged. "Live a little. It's our last summer together, and you're finally single. Everything lined up perfectly. Now let's go. Summer awaits."

Perhaps it was simply the marijuana impairing my judgment, but it didn't take long for me to come around to the idea of leaving the party and going to the beach. Not five minutes had passed before I was pushing myself up from my seat and walking over to Mom to spin my lie. Her face fell, but she relented.

"Today's about you," she whispered into my ear. "I just want it to be perfect. Whatever you want."

Leaving didn't feel good, but I thanked her and did it anyway. I followed Finley across the park, got into his car, and we were off, speeding toward the beach and the promise of Stop 2 and something to get my mind off Tory. Summer awaited.

"What do you think she's doing right now?" I asked after a few minutes on the road. "Does she even care?"

Finley pushed down on the gas pedal and we accelerated toward our exit. "Don't worry about what you can't control."

His car rattled as we merged into the right lane and coasted off the highway. "She could have at least said something," I continued. "Maybe the outcome would have been the same—but still. Nobody deserves what I got."

"Shows how much she really cared." He swung the car into an open parking spot close to the lake and jerked the keys out of the ignition. "This is who she is."

"Three years down the drain."

"Look on the bright side—"

"There is no bright side."

He pushed his door open and stepped outside. Reluctantly, I did the same. We circled the car on opposite sides and stood behind the trunk shoulder-to-shoulder. "Chicago's full of girls, and so is Northwestern. You'll find a new one by the end of Welcome Week, I'm sure of it."

"I doubt that."

"You just have to be willing to try."

"Tory was my soulmate."

Finley pulled the keys back out of his pocket and popped the trunk. He shook his head, then bent down and pulled out two towels. One went under his left arm. The other soared through the air toward my outstretched hand. I caught it. "Soulmates don't do what she did," was all he said.

His words made perfect sense, but that didn't change the fact that I didn't want to believe them. I couldn't believe them. So I hung my head low and stared at the concrete as we walked. My bare feet burned in unison with my heart.

"Try having a good time. Ride out the rest of this high in comfort. Enjoy it. You can worry about Tory and whatever might come next tomorrow."

I shook my head begrudgingly, sighed, and followed him across the parking lot. We stepped together onto the sand. His marijuana hadn't been so bad. I began to wonder if getting drunk would be the same, if it was what I needed to start feeling better and get over Tory.

We continued walking up and down the sandy slopes of the dunes until we reached the big one that separated Stops 2 and 3. The space between the two Stops was a lawless sort of no-man's-land where strangers met and booze flowed freely, the type of place where you could fall in and out of love ten times by noon, where middle-aged divorcees and fresh high school graduates could drink and party with yuppies. Everyone was perpetually drunk and oblivious, loving life under the sweltering heat of the summertime sun in Northern Indiana.

Finley led me all the way up. When we reached the top, he held a hand over his eyebrow, squinted, and began searching for an open space to place our towels.

There were a couple of people nearby, but the majority of them were on the other side, too busy partying and hooking up to pay us any attention. We tossed our towels down a few feet away from the madness and flattened them against the sand before sitting down. Finley pulled an already-open bottle of Jack from his bag and tossed off the top.

"Have some," he said, passing me the bottle after taking a healthy swig himself. "Time to get this summer started."

I shrugged and took it. There was nothing stopping me, so why not? What did I have to lose? I had spent the last three years watching Finley have the time of his life while I played the sober voyeur on the sidelines with Tory, always wanting to join in but never having the courage to actually step forward. I was always scared to take the first shot, to begin. But not anymore. The bottle rose slowly to my lips. It was warm.

The whiskey tasted horrible going down, igniting my throat and sending my face running in a thousand directions at once. I'm sure I looked incredibly stupid, like a lightweight and a fool. But after the fiasco at graduation, I couldn't bring myself to care. Nothing would ever compare to the entire school laughing at me as the banner constricted. Nothing would ever come close.

Finley whooped, cheering me on and bringing me back to my whiskey-tainted reality. Smiling up at the warm blue sky, I decided to push the moment and showed the sun the bottom of the bottle and let a second helping of the foreign liquid tumble down my throat like a desperate waterfall.

The second swallow went down much easier than the first, yet still burned mercilessly. I handed the bottle back to Finley and we went back and forth for a while. Cyclical shots until neither of us could take it anymore. I smiled up at the sky and rested my back against the towel.

Warmth flowed up from the sand and radiated in every direction from below. The world spun.

Up and down, side to side, back and forth.

3

Sweat painted large, dark circles on my shirt that surrounded my armpits. I had no idea how long I'd been asleep for, but the towel was damp when I woke up, and the world wasn't spinning as much as it had been before. I was in a dazed flutter. My head pounded.

"I wonder what he's thinking down there," spoke a woman's voice that sounded like it was coming from above. "He looks so happy. Or maybe he's drunk. I don't know."

"Couple pulls of Jack and he's out cold," said another. It was a voice I immediately recognized. It was Finley, and he was laughing. "It's been about three hours now."

"A couple pulls?" the girl asked. "Is that it? *That's* all it took to knock him out?"

"What can I say? He's a lightweight."

I opened my eyes and sat up. My back was stiff, yet I still managed to smile through the pulsating headache. "This lightweight has a name, you know."

"How're you feeling?" Finley asked.

The girl bent down and handed me a bottle of warm water. I shrugged and took a drink. "Great," I replied. "What'd you guys do while I was out?"

"This one spent the last two hours ogling frat boys on the

other side of the dune," the unnamed girl said. She laughed and threw an arm around Finley's shoulder. "Isn't that right?"

"Shut up."

"Don't go getting bashful now." The girl spun, turning in my direction. We locked eyes. They were brown and slightly bespeckled. "You should've seen this guy back there. It was like he'd known them his entire life."

Finley shook his head, cheeks bright red. "No, no. It wasn't like that, not at all. They were just telling me what life's like at IU. You know, giving me an idea of what to expect when I rush."

"Sounds like you were living your dream."

"We talked about the different houses and which ones I should avoid. That's all."

"Like I said, it sounds like you were living your dream. Joining a frat's all you've talked about since middle school."

He laughed and continued shaking his head.

"I told him to get their numbers," the girl said. "But no, he wouldn't listen. We walked away empty handed."

"Why didn't you?" I asked.

"You were up here sleeping alone and I—"

"Was just too nervous," the girl interjected. "It's okay. We all get scared sometimes."

"I wasn't scared."

"Go back then."

Finley opened his mouth to protest, but the new girl beat him to the punch. "I'll stay here with him and make sure he doesn't do anything drunk and stupid," she said, shoving him toward the frat boys. "Don't even *think* about coming back until you've got at least one of their numbers."

Slowly, he staggered away. "Here goes nothing."

Once he was out of the sight, the girl sat down on the edge of my towel. Her shirt was tied up in a high knot that left most of her stomach exposed. It was redder than Finley's face. I looked into her eyes and saw they looked familiar. I knew her somehow, yet couldn't quite remember how, or what her name was.

She had definitely been a cheerleader, once upon a time. Captain of the Long Beach squad, I remembered that much for sure. The memory of her leading the pep block during my freshman year was etched into my brain. She'd been the pretty senior the whole school stared at apishly during basketball games.

"You went to school with us, didn't you?"

The girl pulled a pack of cigarettes from her jean shorts, took one out, and let it rest on her lips while she fumbled in her other pocket for a lighter. "Yeah, that's right. I graduated a few years before you guys."

"I thought I remembered seeing you at the games."

"That was me." She sighed and took a drag. "The cheer captain dating a wannabe rockstar, the perfect cliche."

Her left leg brushed against mine as she situated herself on my towel. "What's your name?"

"Louie," I replied, speaking too quickly as I wiped my sweaty hands into the towel. Sand stuck to them. "And you? All I know you as is the cheer captain."

"These days I'm just Kai."

"Kai," I said slowly, letting the name roll over my tongue and fester in the air. My mind raced with the desperation of what to say next. "So what'd you end up doing after graduation? I haven't seen you around."

"That's because I left."

"Why?"

"I was running, running from a lie."

"A lie?" I questioned.

"My life, all of it. I never liked cheerleading much, but it was the only way to make my mom happy and say she was proud of me, so it became my personality until I finally broke and couldn't take it anymore."

"What happened?"

"I left the day after graduation, traveled the country, and didn't come back for nearly two years."

How could somebody leave town without a plan, without any

of the logistics figured out? How did she survive? There were so many questions I wanted to ask, yet somehow managed to condense them all into one word that encapsulated it all, "How?"

"It was pretty easy, actually. Brett and I just got into his car and drove and drove until we found a place worth stopping for."

"Brett?" I asked. "Who's that?"

"My high school boyfriend. The *rockstar*."

"Where'd you go?"

"Everywhere," she replied. "All over the country. Our goal was to see as much as we possibly could, to drive until we ran out of money, then stop, find jobs, and repeat the process until we couldn't take it anymore."

"What was the breaking point? Why did it end?"

"Somebody's full of questions today."

I quickly apologized before burying my face into my palms. I'd overstepped the bounds of our newly formed relationship.

"Don't worry about it." The wind caught loose strands of her hair and blew them in every direction. "Just don't get your hopes up. It's not a very interesting story."

"I'm not looking for an interesting story, only yours."

"We were a couple miles outside of LA when it all went wrong, partying at some low-level producer's house when Brett started talking to this girl whose dad worked at one of the major labels in the city.

"In the blink of an eye, I was reduced to nothing. I stopped existing the moment she said she could get him signed. So he took our car and left me stranded at some random guy's house. It probably took him a week to realize what he'd forgotten, if he even has. Either way, I haven't heard from him since."

"Wow. How'd you get home?"

"I didn't. Not right away, at least." The cigarette in her hand was mostly out, burning a lazy orange as smoke drifted from its end. "I was desperate to forget and get over him, so I went back to the beach and drank for days. When that didn't work out, I hitched a ride to Chicago and caught the train back into town. And now

I'm here, talking to you."

"Your tragedy, my luck."

Kai laughed softly, then flicked her cigarette near our feet. She kicked some sand over to cover it. Everything she did seemed to come effortlessly. She existed on an entirely different plane than me. Her adventure was my reason; she loved the unpredictable, while I craved structure.

My goals were loftier than most—Northwestern, J-school, chasing a beat in the big city—but through meticulous effort and rationality, I had concocted the perfect plan to achieve them all, a plan Tory had tried her best to derail.

"So what comes next?" I asked.

Kai undid her messy bun and let the rest of her hair fall onto her shoulders. She shook it out before answering me, sending thick droplets of water in every direction. The sand was temporarily stained dark before the sun caught on, dried them out, and made it burn yellow again.

"You're looking at it," she said. "This is the life."

"What about when summer's over? What's your plan when the beach gets cold and everyone moves on?"

"There's something to be said about just slowing down and living. I have no idea what tomorrow will bring, but right now it's Long Beach take two. And I'm okay with that."

"You can't do anything here. There's no opportunity."

"Opportunity's never meant much to me."

"Oh, come on. You can't mean that. There has to be something out there that you want. Something you're chasing."

"All this," she replied, gesturing around. "It's enough for me. More than enough to keep me busy. I'm happy."

A gust of wind blew sand across our towel. Kai's hair went flying and covered her left eye completely. But she didn't flinch or move to push it away. We both remained still. She just looked at me and I looked back. Nothing more, yet the sensation was entirely foreign. It was beautiful, true.

"What's yours?"

"My dream?"

"Yeah. What do *you* want out of life? What are you chasing?"

"New York," I said simply. "I want to be a professional journalist in the most important city in the world."

"Of course." She made an elaborate show out of rolling her eyes. "I should have known you're a writer."

Chills ran up my spine and made the hairs on my neck stand tall and rigid; I could hardly contain the excitement bubbling within. I was a writer. For the first time in my life, I was an actual, real writer instead of an eager kid chasing an impossible dream.

"What makes you say that?"

"All these questions," she replied. "It seems like a very writerly thing to do."

"I've never thought of it like that before."

"What're you working on right now?"

Her question caught me off guard. "Well, nothing, of course. I haven't even started college yet. I'm nowhere near ready."

"Not ready?" she asked, perking up. "What's that mean?"

"That's what I'm going to Northwestern for."

"To get you ready to write?"

I nodded.

"I don't understand. What exactly do you need them for?"

"To teach me. They're the best J-school in the country."

"But you're missing the point, even if they're the best school in the—"

"They are," I interrupted.

"Right," she said. "Even so. The point stands. Why aren't you writing now? What's holding you back?"

"Nobody'll take me seriously if I start now. I don't have any credibility. But that'll all change after Northwestern. With them behind me, they'll have to listen."

"Degrees don't write stories, you know. People do."

I looked past her toward the lake. Waves broke awkwardly over the shoreline, tumbling into drunk teenagers and sending them down into the sand. I laughed to myself. If only I could see the world as she did, how much simpler everything would be, then I'd be able to just write and it would all find a way to work itself out and be perfect.

Another wave crashed over the shore. She was wrong. The real world demanded credibility; attention was far too valuable to be given away indiscriminately. I looked for the Chicago skyline in the foggy distance, but it wasn't there. The fog was too thick. But it wouldn't be come fall.

It would all be better come fall.

4

Finley staggered up the dune and slowly came into sight. His hair was a mangled, tangly mess and looked like he had just finished running a super marathon or hiking Kilimanjaro. But no, it had only been a few hours of one-on-one face time with frat boys from the Big Ten. That was more than enough.

Our familiar towels and the promise of bottled water must have looked like the perfect oasis in his spinning reality. A smile exploded across his face when we locked eyes, and he began to jog in our direction.

"Get up!" he demanded once he'd reached us, body swaying with the wind. "We can't be late." He sighed, panting out of breath. "Hurry up—the party."

I laughed and tossed him a warm water bottle. "What're you talking about? We left hours ago. It's probably over by now."

"Not that one," he said irritably. Every word that managed to escape his mouth sounded like a laborious struggle. Whatever they had been drinking, it had clearly been strong and he'd had a lot of it. "Not your party. Mathew's."

"Who's Mathew?"

"Frat boy—IU."

"And this Mathew is throwing a party?"

"Yeah. At his beach house."

"Do you really think it's a good idea to go?" I asked. "You seem pretty drun—"

"We all are," he interrupted. He swayed terribly, much worse than before. "Now get up. Let's go."

I shrugged and looked to Kai. "What do you think?"

"I say go. We've got nothing to lose."

"Alright. Looks like it's settled."

"Hurry up," Finley slurred. "We can't be late."

"They'll be too drunk to notice," I said. My vision went fuzzy around the edges as I rose to my feet. Finley staggered and used my shoulders to steady himself. "You'll fit right in."

Still holding Finley up with one side of my body, I reached down with my free hand and pulled Kai to her feet. The three of us stood next to each other as the sun began its daily descent.

Finley's breath reeked of cheap vodka, yet he smiled even wider than he had when he'd gotten his IU acceptance letter in the mail. I had no clue what he'd done with IU-Mathew and his band of fraternity brothers back on the dune, but it appeared to have had a profound effect on him.

We passed all kinds of people on our journey back to the parking lot. The beach had gotten much busier since we'd arrived. All walks of life were equally represented. Rich or poor, collegiate or drop out, the beach paid no mind; sunshine was just the same either way. The water glistened under the day's final rays. Sunlight broke over the horizon. I smiled. There wasn't a prettier sky in all the Midwest.

When we reached the parking lot, we began rinsing the sand off our feet with the rusted outdoor spigot by the bathrooms. Finley giggled whenever our feet collided, touched, or wiggled against each other. He couldn't keep himself contained.

I shook my head, gave him one last nudge with my foot, then turned the water off and asked for his keys. "You seem like you're still a little drunk."

"A little?" Kai quipped. She chuckled to herself as we both

attempted to guide Finley to the car without getting any more sand on his feet. "This man can hardly stand up."

Finley laughed and staggered in the opposite direction. I grabbed his shoulders, steadied them, and ushered him on. "We're almost there," I said. "Only a few more steps."

He muttered something unintelligible under his breath, yet followed my instructions and made it to the car without incident. Kai opened the door to the backseat and he collapsed inside. I folded his legs and made sure they wouldn't get caught in the door before slamming it shut. Throughout it all, he smiled.

"What are we going to do with him?" I asked Kai as I got into the driver's seat. "A party's the last place he should be going right now, don't you think?"

"Don't worry about it," she replied. "It's summer. I've got some more water and a few granola bars in my bag. Take the longest route you can think of. Let him sober up a bit."

I nodded, then closed the door and slid Finley's key into the ignition. Her plan wasn't a great one—far from foolproof—but it sure beat anything I had.

"Where does this IU-Mathew guy even live?" I asked. Acclimating myself to his car, I adjusted the seat before backing out of the parking lot. "What's the address?"

Finley's turn signal felt awkward in my hand, but it blinked a familiar orange once I figured it out. Kai passed the granola bars back to Finley along with a fresh bottle of water. I turned onto Laguna Drive and accelerated toward the highway.

"He didn't give me one."

"Then how am I supposed to get us there?"

"Look for the white house at the end of Montgomery Street. That's all he said. It should be easy to find."

"What street?" I asked sharply.

"Montgomery."

I glanced back at him over my shoulder as I merged. "Montgomery Street?" I repeated back. "You sure about that?"

"That's what he told me."

I looked up at the rearview mirror and was met with a face of unmitigated confidence. Despite being drunk, Finley seemed to know what he was talking about, so I shrugged and turned the car around, accelerating in the opposite direction.

Montgomery Street was the last place I would have imagined the night would take us, yet the tires kept spinning. The highway waned beneath us. We kept moving forward.

The decadent summer homes of wealthy Chicagoans blurred past the windows as we drove further down Montgomery Street. Each had its own individual style and distinct flavor. I imagined their owners were more or less the same, though. Rich people, jaded by all the money in the world.

"Tell us more about this Mathew character," Kai said. She contorted her body to face us both at once. "We know that he's in a frat—"

"Nope," Finley interjected. "He's not just *in* a frat. He's the president of the best house on campus."

"Summer just started and you're already seducing your way to the top." I looked back into the rearview mirror. "That's bold, even for you."

Finley laughed. "Shut up."

"What's his frat called?" Kai asked.

"Delta Chi. The best on campus."

"Is that the one you want to join?"

"If they give me a bid, yeah."

"Give you a bid?" I asked. "What's that mean?"

"If they want me."

"Why wouldn't—"

"That's it!" Finley exclaimed suddenly. "That's his house. The white one on the corner—right there!"

It was the only white house on the block. I'd seen it for a quarter mile. "Yeah, I see it," I muttered, pulling over near the curb. Idling, we all took a moment to collect ourselves and bask in its grandeur.

Whatever Mathew's parents did for a living, it appeared that they did it very well. The house was situated on a perfect corner lot in the most expensive neighborhood in town. Overlooking the water on three sides, I guessed it was easily worth a few million.

"What a house," Kai said.

Finley sighed, clutching an empty granola bar wrapper in his fist. "We should go," he said. "This was a terrible mistake. I don't belong here. None of us do."

"Don't worry about that," I said, echoing his sentiment about Tory and summer. Still, I couldn't help but worry myself. All the context clues pointed to him being right. We were way out of our element. "Just be yourself. It's all you can do."

Meaningless platitudes didn't mean much, but they were enough to earn a quick, tight nod from him before we all stepped out of the car. Kai made eye-contact over the roof and offered a reassuring smile in Finley's direction. I prayed he would get his bid come fall. It would crush him if he didn't.

Finley knocked hard upon reaching the door. It swung open on his third hit, revealing a short, squat young man on the other side. He wore a pale, light blue polo with a complementary white hat. Turned backward, of course.

"You made it!" the squat boy exclaimed before wrapping Finley into a tight hug. When they broke free, he introduced himself to me and Kai in a much more subdued manner, then invited the three of us to come inside.

The inside of his house was a stark contrast from its stately exterior. Everywhere I looked, I saw faceless individuals yelling and dancing and grinding against each other to the beat of terribly mediocre music. The walls shook. None of them cared.

I looked over to my left and saw an uncountable number of generic white boys donning Patagonia t-shirts and pastel short shorts. The universal frat boy uniform of summer. My right saw their numbers doubled with girls; anything to keep the Holy Ratio intact. It was hard to be too judgmental, though. They all looked like they were having the time of their lives, drunk out of their minds, making decisions they would surely regret come morning.

Unsure how to act—I'd never been to a party before, let alone one filled with frat boys and sorority girls—I told Mathew that I loved his house, that it was the most beautiful thing I'd ever seen or been inside. Finley jabbed me hard in the ribs.

"Thanks," he replied, blushing. "Want a tour?"

"A tour sounds great," Kai said, stepping in to save me from myself. Finley covered his face with the palms of his hands and sighed a grateful release. "We'd love one."

Mathew nodded and led us through the living room to the kitchen and showed us the layout of the ground floor. There were three bedrooms, two baths, a back porch, and a grand staircase leading up and down to even more.

He encouraged us to join the rest of the party. "There's food and alcohol all over," he said with a sense of finality. "Take whatever you want. Help yourselves."

Two of Mathew's drunker brothers stumbled over and grabbed him by the shoulders, declaring something incoherent about beer pong. Mathew nodded, smiled, and grabbed Finley's hand, whisking him away before we could say a word.

And we were alone, Kai and I, in a mansion full of strangers on Montgomery Street. What had my life become?

"Don't think we'll be seeing much of him tonight," I mumbled into her ear.

She nodded, laughing.

"What should we do now? This night is hopeless. I'm the DD, so I can't even drink."

"Well I need another cigarette. Let's go outside."

"Lead the way."

Kai gave me a small nod before retracing the path Mathew had just taken. We walked through the kitchen again and passed three separate couples violently making out along the way. My buzz from the beach had fully worn off.

The porch felt like an entirely different world. Everything went quiet when we stepped outside. The blaring, reverberating bass from the music inside the house was a soft drum in the wind's band. Kai propped herself up against the railing.

Her shirt rode up as she dug into her pocket. She pulled out a pack of sandy Marlboro 72s, then a dark blue gas station Bic. She rested one of the 72s on her bottom lip, cupped her hands around it and gave it a light. "Want one?"

"Sure," I replied, shrugging in a way I hoped looked nonchalant. "Why not?"

Half an hour was all it had taken to turn the soft, almost melodic breeze of the beach into a harsh back-and-forth between the trees and waves. They fought against each other, like a set of disobedient twins vying for wombly dominance. And I was the third child, desperately out of place as I struggled to light my first ever cigarette.

The cigarette felt foreign between my lips. It looked effortless when she had done it, yet I couldn't seem to get the light to take. How had she gotten the flame to stay still and ignite?

"This your first time?" Kai asked through a drag. She leaned forward, pulled the Bic back out, and gave me a light. "It looks like you're handling a bomb over there. Don't make me responsible for destroying your lungs."

My cheeks burned. I felt like such a fool as I pulled the cigarette out of my mouth and let out a virginal puff of smoke. It wafted slowly over our heads. "Really, that obvious? I thought for sure I had you fooled."

"Not quite," she said, laughing as she ashed off the edge of the railing. "You can put it out if you want. I won't judge."

"No, no. It's all good. I like it, I think."

She laughed. "Whatever you say."

We settled into a routine: Kai would take an effortless drag, then I would do my best to replicate. This process repeated itself until we'd burned through our two cigarettes. She pulled out a second for herself, but I'd had my fill. "One's good for me."

"So you're a writer," she said after a while, huddling into herself in order to protect the cigarette from the wind's snapping fingers. It took several attempts, but it finally took; its end burned a soft orange. "How'd that happen?"

I didn't know what to say, so I shifted my weight against the railing and looked out over Mathew's backyard and said nothing at all. The grass was freshly cut and led seamlessly into the sand of the Great Lake.

"Who inspires you?" she probed.

"Hunter S. Thompson," I replied instinctually. "No question. He's the best at what I want to do. Fake stories spun from reality. Truth in its truest form."

"Never heard of him before. Did he write anything popular that I would have heard of?"

"*The Rum Diary*'s my favorite book of his, but *Fear and Loathing in Las Vegas* is by far his most famous. Both of them got made into Johnny Depp movies. Have you seen them?"

"Maybe, but I can't remember."

"You wouldn't forget."

Kai took another drag, then flipped her cigarette's smoldering butt over the railing. The tip burned a pale orange until it hit the ground and sputtered out lifelessly. "Is he the reason you want to go to Northwestern?"

"I don't think he went to college."

"Oh, how it feels to be right."

"I'll bite. Go on."

"Remember what I said earlier?"

I nodded.

"If this Hunter S. Thompson guy that you look up to so much can do it without going to Northwestern, why can't you?"

"Yeah, but I'm no Hunter S. Thompson. People like him only come around once or twice a generation."

"You'll never know until you start writing."

I shook my head. She didn't understand.

5

Finley must have uttered the word "Mathew" and some variation of the phrase "once I'm at IU" a thousand times by noon the next day. Drunk or sober, it didn't matter one bit. After treading water for years, he'd finally found himself hooked through the bottom lip without hope of getting away.

"Do you think he liked me?" he asked yet again. He was sprawled out across the couch in his basement while an old basketball game played on the TV behind. "Or was I too drunk? Did I look stupid? You were sober, what'd you think?"

"That it was a party full of frat boys," I replied. "Everybody was drunk."

Finley sighed. "I hope he liked me."

"He wouldn't have invited you if he didn't like you."

"Maybe he was just trying to make numbers. Fill the house with people so the party looks better—optics, you know."

"I don't know about that one. Kai and I aren't really their target demographic."

"You guys came in clutch. Thanks for being the D.D."

"It got my mind off Tory."

"That's the spirit."

"And I got to hang out with Kai some more. She seems pretty

cool. It was a nice, much needed distraction."

"Yeah, she does seem pretty cool," he said, smirking. "I saw you guys left together. What'd you end up doing?"

"Nothing really. We just went outside and smoked, talked until it was time to bring your drunk ass home."

"Smoked?" he questioned. "Twice in one day? Am I hearing you right?"

Reluctantly, I nodded.

"Wow. I never would've thought you had it in you."

"It wasn't marijuana this—"

"Marijuana?" He cackled. "What are you, fifty?"

"Sorry. It wasn't *weed* this time."

"Not better," he laughed. "The thought of you smoking a cigarette is hilarious. Did you like it?"

"Hated every second of it."

"Why'd you do it, then?"

"Couldn't know unless I tried."

Finley's laughter stopped all at once. He sat up on the couch and looked over at me stoically. "Oh, I see. That's it."

"It's nothing like—"

"Yeah, yeah," he interrupted. "Whatever. Of course it's not. So did you get her number or not?"

My eyes slid to the floor. I shook my head.

"Guess who did."

I looked up. "When—"

"Right after we met," he explained. "At the beach, while you were out cold sleeping off the Jack we drank."

"Doesn't matter anyway. I don't need it."

"It can't hurt to save it in your phone. Who knows, maybe you'll want it one day."

My palms began to sweat with anxiety. It felt deeply unnatural to think about another girl and imagine hypotheticals about being with her, like I was cheating despite being single.

"Alright, now it's your turn."

"What's up?"

"Did you get Mathew's number at the party? You were all over each other."

"As a matter of fact, I did."

"And?"

"I haven't texted him yet."

"Why not?"

"Nobody likes a clinger."

"It's a little early in the game to be worried about coming off clingy. If he gave you his number, that means he wants you to text him. Just don't go overboard and you'll be fine."

Finley stood up and began pacing the room. He wrang his hands over each other with every step. Nervous energy radiated palpably from his body. I had never seen him so worked up. The stakes had been irreversibly raised, I feared.

"How about we do it together?"

He looked on, confused.

"We text them both at the same time," I elaborated. "That way we suffer together."

Suddenly, Finley's pacing stopped. He stood in front of the TV, frozen in place, and mulled over my proposition. "Deal," he said after an arduous minute. "Let's do it."

"Now I just need her number. And something to say."

Finley sat next to me on the couch, pulled his phone out of his pocket, and tossed it onto my lap. I turned it over and began scrolling through his contacts.

"Don't overthink it," he advised. Sweat dripped down from my palm and stained the screen, making it difficult to scroll. "Ask her to coffee or something. You can't get rejected if you play it simple. Keep it in public."

"Keep it in public?" I questioned. "Why?"

"First dates should *always* be kept in public."

"But it's not a date."

"What if she thinks it is?"

"Fine. I'll take her to the Peter Cat."

"Wasn't that your go-to spot with Tory?"

"I shouldn't have to stop going there just because she dumped me. That's not fair."

"True, but aren't you worried about running into her? That sounds horrifically awkward if you ask me."

I laughed, but nothing was funny. "She always hated going, said it was dirty and looked cheap—beneath her."

"Oh, well, it looks like you've got it all figured out."

"Everything except what to say."

"Tell her how you feel."

I stared down at my phone for a long time before drafting my first message. I knew Finley was right. You can never go wrong with the truth told in its simplest form, even Hemingway would agree. But what was the truth? How did I feel? The last time I had hung myself out on a limb was when I asked Tory out. She said yes, but look how it ended. A repeat affair would be the death of me.

Hey, I typed. *This is Louie, from the beach. Finley (the drunk one obsessed with frat boys) gave me your number. I was wondering if you wanted to hang out sometime.*

"There you go," I said, tossing my phone onto the vacant cushion between us. "Done. Now it's your turn. Time for you to text Mathew."

Finley groaned, sulking into the couch. Then he began typing. I couldn't read what the message he was composing said, but after a minute or so he suddenly tossed it next to mine and threw his arms over his head. "Now we wait," he groaned.

I sighed and nodded in agreement. But before we could get settled in, the cushion shook with the anxious vibrations of a quick response. All was forgotten. We dove toward them both.

His lock screen remained barren. Mine did not.

Sounds good to me, read her first message. A second quickly came through, followed by a third. *Yesterday was the most fun I've had all summer. What do you want to do?*

"Told you it was a good idea," Finley said, climbing halfway onto my lap so he could read what she'd said. "What are you going to say back?"

"I'm just going to talk to her like I would anybody else, treat her like a normal person." I shifted my body away from his to type out my response without a critique of every word in real-time.

I smiled down at my phone and began composing my response: *What do you think about coffee? I know the best place in town. Does seven tomorrow night work for you?*

"Look at you all smiley over there. Finally moving on from Tory. This is going even faster than I thought."

"Don't get carried away. That's not what this is."

"Yeah, yeah. Sure, of course it's not."

"I'm serious. We're just two kind-of-friends who might end up getting coffee together for an hour or two maybe. That's not moving on. It's not anything at all."

"Whatever you say."

My phone vibrated. Instinctually, I glanced down at her text on my lock screen. *Works for me. I'm free all day.*

I quickly thumbed an affirmation back, then asked Finley what his plan was with Mathew. "Where are you taking him?"

"Who knows if he'll even respond?"

"After last night, me. I'm sure of it."

Before we could bicker further, his phone vibrated and he threw himself off the couch in a struggle to read what it said in private. The color drained suddenly from his face. What followed was an incredibly telling sequence of events: terror, unfulfilled nervous energy, then a display of adulation unlike anything I'd ever seen before.

"He wants to see me tonight. Apparently, he's been wanting to text me all day but couldn't think of what to say."

"Relax," I said. His fingers shook and trembled against my back. "Take your own advice. Play it cool and you'll be fine."

He groaned.

"Looks like somebody can dish it out but can't take it back." I stood up from the couch and took a step toward the door. "You better not back out."

"Where do you think you're going?"

"It's Thursday night. Where do you think?"

"No way you can skip?"

"Not after ditching the grad party," I replied. "Mom looked heartbroken when I told her we were leaving. I can't do that to her again, not so soon after."

"I get that. Well, have fun with Andy."

"Text me later," I said, lingering in the doorway. Desperately, I wanted to stay. "Let me know how things go with Mathew."

"You got it."

The door waved through the frame behind me as I began ascending the stairs, headed toward the promise of Uncle Andrew and yet another family dinner I didn't want to attend.

• • •

The thought of meeting Kai at the Peter Cat kept my mind occupied on my drive home. Calling it a date felt disingenuous, bordering on an outright lie. Dates had been intrinsically linked with Tory for as long as I could remember. It would take much more than a day to reboot and restructure my brain's internal programming.

A couple of cars driven by presumed businessmen—if they weren't, they certainly looked the part—roared off the highway and passed me, honking their horns as they did. But I held a steady forty-five until I was on the back roads leading to my house. I was in no hurry; they could wait.

Uncle Andrew's car was parked in my spot when I pulled up, forcing me to park on the side of the road. It annoyed me more than it should have. He knew exactly where I usually parked, so it felt intentional.

Our weekly Thursday dinners were like clockwork. They long predated my license, and I'd always hated them. But I vowed to remain quiet and let it go. Anything to get the evening over with quickly, to get him in and out, just like always.

I walked inside. The door slammed behind me.

"Look who decided to finally show up," proclaimed Uncle Andrew as I stepped through the doorway. "My favorite nephew. Fashionably late, as always."

Mom jumped off the loveseat next to him and pulled me into a hug, laughing as she did. "Sorry I'm late," I mumbled.

"Don't worry about it. It's summer vacation. Slightly late is right on time if you ask me."

I laughed. Uncle Andrew pulled me away from her clutches and into a hug of his own. He patted me on the back before rubbing small, methodic circles into it. "What's for dinner?" I asked, turning my head away to meet Mom's gaze.

"Roast beef and those little red potatoes you love."

"Sounds good. Is it done yet?"

"Looks like someone's hungry."

I smiled, nodding.

"Let me go check on it," she said, then walked away and left me and Uncle Andrew in the living room together, alone.

"What have you been up to lately?" he asked after she was comfortably out of ear shot. "It feels like forever since we've had a good chat or any time alone. I miss you so much."

"Sorry. I've been busy with school stuff. Between graduation and figuring out college, I haven't done much of anything."

"Besides partying at the beach," he replied, smirking. "Yeah, your mother told me all about what you did."

"It's a school tradition. Everybody went."

"Hmm," he said slowly, dragging the noise out as he looked me over. "I guess I'll let it slide this time," he continued, his voice measured and deliberate. "Is that where you were today?"

I took a step back, away from him in the direction of the kitchen. "No, I was at Finley's. We were hanging out and watching TV and I lost track of time."

"Who's Finley?"

"My best friend. You had him in your class."

"Same year as you?"

I nodded.

"Oh, well that explains it. That year was such a blur. You're all I can remember."

Mom shouted from the kitchen. We couldn't understand what she was saying over a timer going off, but the sentiment was clear enough: dinner was ready. And more importantly, our conversation over. We followed her voice and the scent of freshly cooked roast beef and sat down around the table.

I told her it all looked incredible.

"It really does," Uncle Andrew agreed, sitting down himself. "You really outdid yourself tonight, Ava."

A smile exploded across her face. She stuffed our plates and passed them around the table. I took a deep, slow breath inward. It all smelled excellent, perfectly cooked. If I had to suffer through two more months of weekly family dinners with Uncle Andrew, at least I knew the food would be good.

I had only taken five or six bites before the beautifully scented silence was broken and Uncle Andrew began questioning me about Northwestern. "You must be so proud," he said in Mom's direction. "It's a very competitive school. All that good parenting's finally starting to pay off."

"Everything Louie does makes me proud," she replied. "But I can't take all the credit, raising him was a group effort. It really does take a village. There's no way we could've done it without a certain third-grade teacher taking a special interest in him."

A long, sly smile eroded cancerously across Uncle Andrew's face. He merely shrugged. "I did what anyone would with a kid like Lou. He's an easy one to love."

I said nothing.

Mom jabbed me with her elbow under the table. Her eyes burned into the side of my head, silently demanding I speak up and thank him. Then she kicked me again, hard. My shin seared with pain. "Thanks," was all I could manage.

Uncle Andrew smiled, stretching himself over the table to rub his hand over mine. "You must be so excited for the big city. You'll be unrecognizable the next time I see you."

Mom sighed and buried her face into her palms. "Today's been so good. Let's not ruin it by talking about stuff like that. Nobody wants to see me crying."

"Here, here," Uncle Andrew said. "Only positivity from here on out."

I pulled my hand away from Uncle Andrew's and rubbed it on top of Mom's. It was ice cold, trembling. "Don't worry about me leaving," I whispered. "Evanston's just a train ride away. I'll be home all the time."

Her upper lip steadied. "You better."

"Of course. All the time."

"What about me?" Uncle Andrew asked. His voice was loud and light, the complete opposite of hers. He grinned widely as he dug into another bite of roast beef. "Won't you miss me too?"

My grip tightened around my fork.

"Don't go forgetting about me."

"How could I?"

6

It took the better part of forty-five minutes to traverse the barren roads separating my house from Kai's. My palms were pressed firmly against the steering wheel, fingers tapping rhythmically against the leather. Up down, up down, up down. I drove through the Uptown Arts District and headed toward the suburbs.

I passed the entrance to her cul-de-sac three times before conquering my fear and turning in. Everything had been so simple at the beach. There were no expectations, no pressure of a maybe-date or anything else. Just fun, drunken spontaneity. Talking to her sober and alone terrified me.

Her house sat in the middle of the main loop. It was the epitome of average. Not too big, but not too small either. There was a thoughtful, well-manicured garden out front, full of vibrant petunias, daisies, and rhododendrons, all in full bloom.

I smiled at their beauty and parked near the curb, idling a while before texting her. *I'm here,* I wrote. *Look outside.* Several long seconds labored past before her living room curtains suddenly ripped open and her freckled face poked out between them.

She ran outside; my heart raced. She looked beautiful.

"I thought you'd gotten lost," she said, sitting down next to me in the passenger's seat. "You had me worried."

"Traffic was terrible." It wasn't. I was just scared.

"Oh, well, at least you're here now."

I smiled and shifted the car back into drive. The engine rumbled as I pulled away from the curb.

"Soo," Kai began, contorting her face in all kinds of mockingly thoughtful ways. "Where are we going? You said you know the best place in town, but never where."

"It's a surprise. Have a little faith."

"Give me a hint."

"Hm, alright. It's a place you've never been."

"Now how could you possibly know that?"

"Trust me, I used to go there all the time with—"

My eyes widened twice their usual size as the rest of my body caught on to the words that nearly escaped my lips. I clinched my fists around the wheel, veins nearly popping out of my arms.

"Go ahead," she encouraged. "Finish what you were about to say. Whatever it is, I promise it won't hurt my feelings."

"I—"

"You can trust me," she said firmly.

"I used to go there with Tory."

"Who's Tory?"

I sighed. "My ex."

"Interesting."

"I only said it—"

"You don't have to explain anything," she interrupted. "Not to me, at least. We're not together."

"So you're not mad?"

"Not at all," she replied. "Nobody will ever get to know the real you if you hide your past."

I smiled, but struggled to believe her fully. We passed the sign for the Uptown Arts District in relatively amicable silence. Somebody had spray-painted over some of its letters in the winter, and the city had yet to fix the eyesore. I drove deeper into it until we were parked in front of the Peter Cat.

The Peter Cat was a quaint cafe, tucked away on the bottom

floor of an old, two-story brutalist warehouse that had been poorly converted, and certainly seen much better days. It was the type of place that every truly Midwestern city had, a combination of old classic Americana glory that stunk with the beautiful stench of the dream immigrants believed and chased furiously. But for whatever reason, they never worked out, their dreams died, and they never made it. Where their dreams died, the Peter Cat was born.

"What happened between you and Tory?" Kai asked suddenly. The car was turned off, and the keys were out of the ignition, resting in my hand. "Was it a recent thing?"

"Two days ago. About five hours before we met."

Kai looked me over with an undecipherable face. It was impossible to tell whether the creases in her forehead were caused by pity, strain, or something else entirely. "Were you serious?"

"Very. We dated all through high school."

She put a hand over her heart. "Wow. That hurts."

"Nothing I can do about it now."

"You could always tell me how you feel," she suggested. "Whatever that is. It doesn't have to lead anywhere. Just let everything out. See where that takes you."

"What's the point? It won't change anything. Nothing can. What happened, happened. And now it is what it is."

"Spoken like a true nihilist."

"Well, it's true."

"Life's hardly ever that simple."

I stared ahead through the window. The Peter Cat was completely empty. "Do you still want to do this?"

"Of course. Why wouldn't I?"

"Oh, I don't know. I thought bringing up my ex might have made you uncomfortable and that you wanted to go home."

"Whatever happened between you guys is what molded you into who you are today, the guy I met at the beach. And I liked that guy, so I'm okay with whatever it took to make him."

We looked at each other before getting out. "Still, we should be taking about something happier, something lighter than my terrible breakup."

Kai laughed. I slammed my door shut. "I'd rather talk about something uncomfortable that's real than lie and live somewhere that doesn't exist, even if it's beautiful."

The more I interacted with Kai the more I realized she was completely antithetical to Tory and everything our relationship stood for. Communicating with her was a back-and-forth. Still, it was hard for me to adjust to the change in real-time. I couldn't help but long for the familiar.

When we reached the Peter Cat's front entrance I lingered and gestured toward their sign on the corner. "The best coffee shop in Long Beach," I said. "Welcome to the Peter Cat."

Kai looked the building up and down with squinted, questioning eyes. It looked nothing short of shabby, I knew that just as well as she did, but I also knew that its true beauty existed beneath the cracked bricks and dirt-covered windows.

"This is it?" she asked. The muscles in her cheek worked overtime in an effort to keep her face straight. "*This* is the best coffee shop in Long Beach?"

"Wait until you're inside. The place sneaks up on you. You'll be a regular before you know it. Mark my words."

Kai laughed and shook her head. I opened the door. An audible groan accompanied her first step into the cafe. While she saw a sagging counter covered in mysterious stains, a coffee shop without customers, I saw Long Beach in its truest and most authentic form, raw and unashamed.

The bitter scent of strong, freshly brewed tea billowed over the pages of the book the girl behind the counter read. She was the owner's beloved granddaughter, and worked the cafe whenever he was out. Smiling, she looked up at us and refilled her cup.

We took a step further and saw the owner's bookshelf packed full of his most prized possessions. French masters like Camus and Hugo sat next to Houellebecq, the country's modern enfant terrible. There were even a few Japanese imports tucked away by the cash register. Those were his favorites.

On my first date with Tory, he had hobbled over to our table and given me a shabby translation of *Story of the Eye* before walking away, giggling manically behind the counter as he looked on. I had no idea what was going on at the time, but when I got home I burned straight through the twisted novella and quickly understood. When done correctly, words can be so much more than entertainment. They're the only thing that can immortalize a man, forever brand his story into the fabric of time.

Looking up from her book, the girl behind the counter immediately recognized me. Her smile grew as she ripped a few basil leaves off the plant behind and threw them in her cup. "What can I get for you today?" she asked. "The usual?"

I nodded and slid my card across the counter. "That, and whatever she wants, please."

Kai ordered a small mocha latte with an extra shot of espresso. The girl nodded, then swiped my card through the machine. Her movements were without thought. Working at the Peter Cat was all she'd ever known. It was all she would ever have. Suddenly sad, I gave her a three dollar tip and turned away.

The interior of the coffee shop was small and cramped, so seating choices were limited even when it was empty. There were a few chairs by the bookshelf, a lopsided table for two in the center of the room, and a small booth tucked under a window facing the busy sidewalk outside. Tory's name and face were etched into all of them. Her laugh, our love, all of it. Top to bottom, down to every last brick. The choice was obvious. I sighed and led us to the booth by the window.

A few cars drifted past sporadically, headlights dotting the black night. Kai rested her hands on the table and looked me in the eyes. "You seem off," she muttered. "Want to talk some more about the girl from before?"

"I'm sorry," I sighed. "I'm just caught up in my head right now, that's all. Don't worry. I'll snap out of it soon."

"You don't have to snap out of anything," she said. "Just talk. I'm here to listen."

"I can't—no. Not right now."

"That's okay. It's up to you. We can talk about her or you or something else entirely, I don't mind. Whatever you want."

The owner's granddaughter approached our booth and set our drinks down on the table—a café crème for me, mocha extra shot for Kai—then briskly walked away and returned to her book. Silence came over the table in her absence.

"I want to be here with you right now." Kai's smile disappeared behind the first sip of her coffee. "But I can't get her out of my head and I don't know why. It's confusing."

"I understand. I missed Brett all the time at first—"

"Brett?" I interrupted.

"The guy I told you about the other day. You know, the one that ran off and left me alone in LA."

"Oh yeah, right."

"Anyway, it took me months to stop obsessing and praying for him to come back and love me."

I took a sip from my coffee. Steam fogged my glasses. "And what about now?" I asked. "Do you still think about him?"

"Hardly crosses my mind."

"I guess I just always thought that we would be different, that we would be the exception to the rule, different than everyone else. For some reason, I always thought we'd make it.

"And that's what tied my whole life together, the consistent thread of her, our plan and what she thought of it. Now that she's gone, I have no idea what to do with myself. I don't know how to move forward without constantly looking back."

Kai reached her hand across the table and rested it on top of mine. The moment didn't feel inherently sexual, just intimate in a way I hadn't experienced before. I smiled as her finger traced my knuckle, tensing slightly.

"Focus on writing," she suggested. "That's what I would do. Forget about this Tory girl and just write as much as you can. Start sending out your work and see what sticks. Chase your dreams. Become a journalist for real."

I scoffed. "If only it was that easy."

"It'll be hard, but so is everything worth doing."

I looked away from her and out the window. An old man bustled past with a bundle of cherry blossoms tucked under his arm. He stopped and waved in our direction. Kai didn't notice.

I didn't react.

7

Much of the next morning was lost berating myself over Tory and what I had done at the Peter Cat. Even though our pseudo-date had gone well enough, I couldn't help but wonder how great it could have been if I would've just kept my mouth shut and not mentioned my heartbreak or ex-girlfriend.

But it was impossible to know for sure, pointless to look back and wonder what if. The future was all I had. A few warm months before I packed my bags and everything changed for good. It was well past noon, and I was still wallowing in my childhood bedroom drunk on self-pity.

Then came three crisp knocks that sent me upright. I propped my back against the headboard and locked my eyes on the door. The knob turned slowly before bursting open.

It was Mom. "Finley's here," she said from the door. "I don't know what he wants, but he said it's important."

Before I could react or even think about getting dressed, Finley took two quick, familiar strides across my bedroom floor and plopped himself down at the foot of my bed.

"What's going on?" he asked, settling near my feet. "How'd things go with Kai last night? You never texted me."

"What about you and IU-Mathew?" I deflected. "Did you

guys hang out after I left?"

Finley blushed, breaking eye contact.

"So there *is* something," I continued emphatically. "Now you have to tell me. Give me all the details."

"It wasn't much of anything, really. We just walked along the waterfront and talked for a few hours."

"Did you make a move?"

"We had the perfect moment to—the sun was setting beautifully across the lake—but I got scared and chickened out, then the moment passed and never came again."

"That's rough. What happened next?"

"Nothing at all. We kept walking and talking and acted like nothing happened, like there hadn't been a moment and I hadn't blown it."

"Maybe you didn't."

"You should've been there. It was terrible."

"Have you talked since?"

Finley nodded. "We've been talking nonstop ever since, but still haven't addressed what happened."

"That's not too bad. Just make sure you make the move next time you hangout since you rejected—"

"I didn't reject him," he interrupted.

"You said you got scared and chickened out," I replied. "*I* know that, but does he? He probably thinks you don't like him."

His eyes fell. Eventually, they settled on the carpet. A sigh escaped his lips. "Yeah, well what about you?" he asked.

"What about me?"

"Did you make a move?"

"Does talking about my ex-girlfriend the entire time count as making a move?"

"No way," he whispered, eyes widening. "You didn't."

"Oh, yes I did. I brought Tory up before we'd even parked, then talked about her more inside."

"Why would you do that?"

"She was all I could think about. I couldn't help myself."

Finley shook his head and rubbed his hand uncomfortably against my knee. "How'd she react? Did she freak out?"

"Much better than I could've hoped for. She told me that I wasn't weird for thinking about my ex, and that she struggled getting over hers too at first, but it got better with time."

"That sounds so awkward."

"It was. But I had a good time anyway. Hanging out with her is fun. I like it."

"Think you will again?"

"I want to, but I don't know if she does."

"Have you been talking?"

"Not a single text."

"Well, have you tried?"

"No. I can't find the words."

"And you're saying I gave mixed signals."

"Or maybe she thinks I'm hung up on Tory."

"Push past that. You have to at least try."

"But that's the problem. I *am* still hung up on Tory."

"Don't you like Kai too?"

"Exactly. That's the problem. I don't know what to do."

"Keep seeing her and let things come naturally. See where the summer takes you, even if it means just being friends. That's what I would do. Tell her you had fun the other day and want to see her again sometime."

I gripped my phone under the blanket and ran my fingers over the back of its case. "Should I apologize?"

"No. Don't mention it again."

I nodded and pulled the phone out. An empty black screen stared back, taunting me silently as I began to type with shaking fingers. *Last night was fun. We should do it again sometime soon.*

"There you go," I said, tossing the phone by my feet. "It's done. I texted her."

Finley smirked. "See, that wasn't so hard."

"Easy for you to—"

My phone vibrated suddenly, interrupting me. I dove across

the bed and flipped it over to read her message. *Me too,* she wrote. *I'm at the beach rn. Come through if you aren't too busy.*

Excitement coursed through my veins as I read her tiny, pixelated message. Finley said something about being right and that I would be over Tory by the end of the week. But I ignored him, and shook my head before jumping off the bed to get ready.

"You don't mind if I leave, do you?" I asked once I'd gotten myself casually presentable, foot twitching.

"Doesn't look like I have much of a choice."

My body tensed as I took an apprehensive step forward. Finley laughed and got off the bed. He pushed me into the hallway with unusual force. "Get out of here," he demanded. "Go to the beach. Go get your girl."

"Not my girl," I replied instinctively. But I had to admit, if only to myself, that there was something different about her. Something special that I couldn't quite put my finger on.

• • •

My pants had barely grazed the leather of my seat before I'd shifted the car into reverse and was halfway out the driveway speeding. Cars honked. Angry drivers flipped me the bird as I bustled past them and roared further down the open road. I pushed the gas pedal to the floor, the engine caught, and I accelerated further. Anything to reach her just one second sooner.

The congested highways wrapped their long-winding tentacles all throughout Long Beach. They looked beautiful in the frenetic blur, combining the florescent lights of local businesses' LED signs and the flickering turn signals of surrounding vehicles into a Pollock only I could see. Everything was beautiful. It all was true and just might work out okay.

My car trembled as I crossed the rumble strip that connected the highway's river to its lush side road tributaries that led to the beach. Another two miles passed by without much thought. I relied on nothing more than instinct as I whipped the car around the last turn and pulled into the parking lot closest to the sand.

Idling, I thumbed Kai a quick text. *Here*, I typed before stepping outside and slamming the car door behind me. The wind smacked my face, whipping me on either side with stray strands of hair. *Where are you?*

I walked down to the coastline and hugged the water until she replied. *I'm at the big dune. Where we first met.*

The water crashed over my feet, chilling my toes. I stared down at my phone and read her response three times over. I'm sure I looked like a fool smiling down at my phone, but I didn't care. In many ways, a fool was exactly what I was. *See you soon.*

It was a little past six when I finally reached the big dune where we'd first met. I smiled to myself, remembering how tired and groggy I'd been when I looked up and saw her for the first time. The beach had been a lot busier that day.

"You found me!" Kai said. She wrapped an arm around me and pulled me tightly into her side. My heart accelerated; I hoped she couldn't feel it.

She stood by herself with a tattered bookbag slung over her shoulder, smiling near a large crowd of drunk, obnoxious, obviously underage teenage girls. They looked like the juvenile, female equivalent of Mathew's band of fraternity brothers.

"Can't get rid of me that easily." I laughed and wrung my hands over each other in a futile attempt to calm my nerves. "Sorry it took me so long to text you after our da—"

"So it *was* a date. I knew it."

Anxiety settled in, but I forced a smile out regardless. I feared that I had overplayed my hand. "Is that okay?"

"Is what okay? Calling it a date?"

I nodded, staring down at the sand between my feet.

"Did you mean it as one?"

"Not entirely," I replied. "But I wish it was."

"Then it was," she said, smiling widely before grabbing my wrist and pulling me closer. "Now let's go. There's something I want to show you."

I stumbled forward in the direction she pulled me and nearly lost my balance in the process. "Where are you taking me?"

"Don't you go worrying about that," she said, continuing to walk, smiling as she did. "Last time you surprised me. This time it's my turn."

Shaking my head, I made the decision to follow her wherever she led. Up one dune, down another, across a third. We repeated this process several times, wading through the drunk masses. She only stopped when we reached the mouth of Elwood Grove. We stood still, staring at each other in the warm summer breeze.

"What're we doing here? Nobody goes to the Grove anymore, not since they shut down the nature center."

"That's what makes it perfect."

"I don't understand."

"Everybody walks right past, never seeing beyond what they've been told. They all think the park's closed because someone with power and a fancy title told them it was. But you can't shut down nature. It goes on whether we want it to or not."

Kai grabbed me by the wrist and drug me forward again, onto the overgrown dirt trails that lead into Elwood Grove. My bare feet crunched and twinged with pain as the soft sand slowly turned to sticks and rocks that were barely visible.

"If you follow the trail we'll be there in no time."

I shook my head and laughed softly into the breeze, praying that our walk would be brief. All I wanted was to get wherever we were going quickly so that my feet could stop hurting and I could talk to her and do all the things I hadn't at the Peter Cat.

But the trails of Elwood Grove had other ideas. The hot sun beat down on the top of my head and neck, sweat bubbling just beneath my skin and causing small gray sweat stains to start forming around my armpits.

The undergrowth grew thicker and more dense with every twist and turn of the trail. After a few minutes, it was invisible, covered completely by sticks and rocks and indecipherable shrubbery. It was easily fifteen degrees cooler beneath the canopy of the forest, a separate world from the scorching beach.

"One more turn," Kai muttered, glancing back at me from ten yards ahead. "One more turn and we're there."

I said nothing. My head dripped, soaking wet from sweat. I heaved forward into the thickening, damp air. The trees began to thin around us. The beach became visible once more. Where we were, I had no idea, just that we'd arrived.

Kai urged me on. We stumbled together through another opening. It was different than the one from before, empty. We were truly alone, inches apart in the untouched microcosm of summer. And it was beautiful.

"Isn't it wonderful?" she whispered.

It truly was. Words would never be able to articulate the emotions coursing through me, so I didn't bother trying. I just stood still and took it all in next to her in blissful, absolute silence. Nothing mattered besides the moment, nobody but her.

She walked to the edge of the clearing and stood on its rocky edge. The loose ends of her bikini straps flapped in the wind and lashed against her peeling skin. I followed suit and did the same. We stood tall together atop the rocks, looking over the crowded beach like the Redeemer did in Rio.

Everything beneath felt inconsequential as we looked down upon it. None of it mattered. It was only us. Everything else was quiet, oddly so. I looked over at Kai and she looked over at me.

"Thanks for bringing me here," I said. "This is a much better surprise than mine was. It's beautiful."

"It's a view I'll never get used to, that's for sure. When the weather's nice and the sky is clear you can see the entire skyline. Chicago's right at your fingertips, so close it feels like one leap is all it would take to land in the Loop."

One leap, I thought to myself, looking out over the water with her. One leap is all that it would take to change everything.

But the fog was heavy, my doubt even more, and we couldn't see a thing either way. It just wasn't the right time.

"There's something beautiful about not being able to see the city yet knowing it's there. Millions of people hidden behind an invisible wall."

Kai's forehead creased. "You're the only person I've ever heard describe it like that. Interesting. I like it." I could feel her breath against the back of my neck with every word she spoke.

The gentle smell of strawberry wafted into my nose. My heart beat through my throat. "When did you find this place?"

The smile on her face went sour, disappearing as quickly as it'd came. "Brett," she whispered over the abyss. "He took me here for our first date."

"That's a much better first date than going to a run-down coffee shop and monologuing about your ex the entire time."

Kai laughed. "It wasn't *that* run-down."

"Look at this."

"I love it."

"Does it remind you of him?"

She sighed and looked away. Her lips remained pressed together, but she didn't say a word. Birds chirped behind us. Radio bangers screamed below. I thought about reaching over and grabbing her hand, but froze and didn't. It felt like too big a step.

"Do you want to head back?" I asked. "We can go do something else if you don't feel comfortable being here."

"No," she said. "I can't run and hide from him and all the memories we share. I have to live life on my terms, not his."

Silence slowly began to creep into the small space between us on our shared rock. The wind picked up. Everything went cold. I looked at Kai. After a few seconds, she looked back at me. "What did you guys do up here?"

"On our first date?"

Reluctantly, I nodded.

She closed her eyes and took a slow, collected breath inward before responding. "He took me up here at sunset one day after a basketball game and played me a song he'd written for me on his guitar. And that was all it took. I was hooked. Hopelessly in love. Two years later I was chasing him across the country."

I nodded before looking away, silently wondering how it had

all gone so terribly wrong between the two of them. What pushed him to leave her alone, desperate in Los Angeles? How did their love manage to drift so far away from where it began? Did he regret what he'd done, or did he not even care?

Maybe their story had been something like mine and Tory's, I imagined. Perfect one day, then suddenly not the next. No explanations or rationale, just the searing pain of an unwanted, ruthless break. There was nothing I could have said or done to change her mind about us at graduation. Going to university in England was her fancy record label. She chose to dream instead of love.

We were over and that was that. I was hopeless. Kai probably felt the same. She relaxed into my body. The fog cleared a bit and we watched the sun fall behind Sears Tower. It became dark quickly after. We were together.

We were alright.

• • •

My car hardly had the chance to start before I was backing it out of the sandy parking lot and rushing toward Cherry Lane, desperate to reach Finley and tell him all about what had happened on the clearing.

A solution to my Tory problem had suddenly presented itself, birthed from nothing at all. The only problem was that it wasn't a solution at all, but rather an entirely new set of questions, accompanied by a vast array of unknown answers. My car barely had the chance to stop before I was halfway to his front door. I pushed it open and plunged inside.

But when I reached the bottom of his staircase, Finley was so tightly wound with visibly encumbering anxiety that I decided against talking about myself, and instead focus on him at first. We would have a much more beneficial conversation that way. I sat down and asked what was going on.

"Mathew invited me to a huge party," he replied, contorting his body to face me directly. "And I have no idea what do."

"He invited you to a party? What's wrong with that?"

"All the brothers will be there."

"I don't understand. Isn't hanging out with a bunch of frat boys the whole reason you're going to IU? This is even better than what you'll get down there. It's at a beach house."

His eyes fell to the floor. "What if I don't pass?"

"How do you 'pass' a party?"

"He won't keep me around if his friends don't like me."

"Isn't he their leader or something?"

"President, yeah."

"See? You've got nothing to worry about. They'll do whatever he does. And since he obviously likes you, so will they."

"Thanks," he said, laughing sardonically as he continued to pace the room in an anxious stupor. "How comforting."

"When is it?"

"Tonight. In half an hour."

"He's invited you to two different parties at his house within the last three days. Don't forget that. It's obvious that he likes you—a lot."

His pacing stopped. "But what if he changes his mind?" Finley asked. He spoke in such a low whisper that I had to strain myself to make out what he was saying. "What if he decides he doesn't like me anymore?"

"Frat boys are a dime a dozen."

"He's different."

It felt weird listening to Finley talk about a boy he had just met with such sincerity, yet it was true. He was, and didn't seem to have any plans of stopping. Whatever it was, I'd never seen it get him before. I imagined it ran much deeper than the fraternity house Mathew belonged to.

I stood up from the couch and wrapped an arm around his shoulder. His muscles were tightly clinched. He fought against my touch in favor of continued pacing, but I held on and refused to let go, just like he had at graduation.

"It's going to be okay," I whispered into his ear. "They're all going to like you. It's all going to be okay. Trust me"

He closed his eyes, sighed deeply through his entire body, and then opened them again to stare at mine. "You don't know that."

"There's only one way to find out."

He sighed. "Wish me luck."

"You won't need it."

I pushed him toward the door. He hesitated near the stairs, and I thought briefly about calling him back to talk about Kai, but decided against it and waved him on instead. Suddenly, I was alone in a house that wasn't my own, so I slid my shoes back on and left myself. A slight breeze had picked up since the beach. But it felt nice, so I embraced it and rolled the windows down.

Warren Zevon sang softly from my speakers as I backed out of Finley's driveway onto Cherry Lane and began heading home. I cruised down the open road and tried making sense of the day I'd just had, but not much sense came to me.

My thoughts tumbled downward, backed by a crooning rendition of "Carmelita" and an Indiana highway riddled with potholes. Few answers came as the road passed beneath, and my brain remained empty as I rolled to a stop in front of my house fifteen minutes later. There was no way to be sure, not about anything.

All I could do was move forward, and hope.

8

Two days passed without much interaction with Finley. We were both still very much in the dark about the other's life, sprinting down the fast lane of our own desires, blinders high, unwavering. It was a position I hadn't expected us to find ourselves in until much later, until after we left for our respective universities. Yet there we were already, less than a week into summer.

The appeal of Kai radiated constantly. It was unknown and overwhelming. I couldn't get the image of her sitting on the rocks of the clearing out of my head. I craved seeing her again. I wanted to squeeze every last drop out of our shared summer.

So I clicked away from Finley's name in my contact list and thumbed her a quick text at the stoplight instead. *I'm about to go to the beach. We should meet up.*

My phone vibrated before I could cross the intersection. *I'm here. Meet me at the clearing.*

I smiled nonsensically to myself before typing out a quick affirmative. My free hand cranked the wheel left and caused my heart to flutter against my sternum. The beach was only a few streets away. Once I crossed them, it would only be a few dunes separating the two of us.

My mind raced with what I would say. How would I react

when I saw her? Did she want me to hold her tight and kiss her passionately, or simply be her friend?

I had no idea the protocol. It'd been years since I had concerned myself with any of the complex rules that surrounded the first move. Getting hitched to Tory at such a young age allowed me to skip over many of them. I was able to bypass the awkward teenage phase everybody fumbles through in high school.

Countless parties separated the sandy parking lot from Elwood Grove and the trails leading up to Kai. A few of the more excitable partiers—or perhaps just the most drunk—offered me shots as I walked past. I ignored them all and continued to move forward. My mind was preoccupied with trying to figure out how I should navigate through the next few hours.

Navigating the twisting trails proved much more difficult without Kai's constant instructions and encouragement. All the trees looked exactly the same; every turn brought another wave.

I closed my eyes and saw two massive green ones staring back at me. They shined, laughing at my foolish audacity. How dare I have hope? My feet remained on a steady trajectory, consistently moving forward, but my mind did not.

Giving up wasn't an option, but doubt and self-loathing surely were. I had to keep going. Miserable, but onward. There were far too many unsolved hypotheticals. I had to find out for myself. So it was decided. One foot after another until the trees thinned.

Kai's silhouette became visible immediately upon crossing the threshold of the clearing. Her back was propped against one of the tall, vertically protruding rocks near the edge. I lingered where I stood, invisible to her, and watched small puffs of smoke rise over her head before dissipating into the air.

"Look who it is," she said, speaking softly as I stepped into view. A burning cigarette rested on the edge of her bottom lip. It bounced with every word she spoke. "I was sure you'd get lost without me."

"I almost did." I laughed as I sat next to her in the sand. "That forest has a mind of its own."

"Or maybe you just weren't paying attention last time," she replied coyly. "Something must have had you distracted."

"Hm. I wonder what that could've been."

She smiled and pulled her hair up into a loose, messy bun. Small pieces stuck out in every direction, but she didn't seem to mind. "I've got something that will make this night a whole lot better," she said, clutching her bookbag.

"Three for three with the surprises."

She turned the bag upside down and dumped its contents out onto the sand. First came a small roll of plastic cups, then a pack of cigarettes, and, finally, the Holy Grail—an entire bottle of obviously cheap vodka.

"Tell me this won't make things more interesting."

Sweat bubbled under my skin, struggling against the sealed valves of my pores, desperate to break free. I'd never been properly dunk before, but didn't know how articulate my inexperience without looking like a loser in front of the former cheer captain. I glanced around the clearing for something to latch onto, but there was nothing. Everything was barren all the sudden.

"Grab a cup," she instructed. "What do you say? Let's toast and get this night going."

My vision began to blur from the corner of my eyes moving inward as she poured a cup full of vodka and motioned for me to do the same. The bottle felt so slippery in my shaking hands, so out of place and foreign, much worse than the blunt or cigarettes had before. "I don't know," I finally managed. "Maybe this isn't the best idea tonight."

Kai crossed her legs and held my cup steady. "Why not?" she asked. "Don't worry about how it tastes. You'll hardly notice once we're a few shots in."

"I can't drink and drive."

She sighed a sigh of release before grabbing my hand and filling my cup up for me. "Then don't," she said as the cup filled with more vodka. "That's an easy problem to solve."

"How so?"

"You stay here. Stay here and get drunk with me tonight. We can sleep under the stars and wake up with the sun."

As tempting as her offer sounded, I couldn't take her up on it in good faith. If I did, it would only be a matter of time before my inexperience showed. I would drink too much and tell her everything. And once she knew about the green eyes and what came with them, we would be ruined. Over before we had a chance to ever properly begin.

She'd see me for the freak I truly was. A halfway man who couldn't get over the past. So I shook my head and blamed the weather. "It gets cold by the water at night," I said. "We'll freeze once the sun goes down."

"I've got an old jacket in my bag. We can sleep under that. I'll even let you cuddle me if you get too cold."

"Alright," I said reluctantly, trying my best to appear excited despite the swelling anxiety that coursed through my veins. "Looks like it's settled then. We're sleeping outside."

"Nothing's better than looking out over the lake before the sun comes up. When nobody else is around, it's like the world is yours and yours alone."

"Now all we need is some shots." I hated how forced it sounded coming out of my mouth, but Kai didn't appear to notice. If she did, she didn't say anything.

"On three?" she asked.

I nodded and held my plastic cup out. It clinked softly against hers. My hand shook with nervous anxiety. "You never get used to the taste of this stuff," she said once she'd swallowed, face contorted in every direction.

"Then why do you drink it?"

"Because it's cheap and gets me where I'm trying to go."

I sighed and downed mine silently, eyes wide open. My brain was locked on one thing and one thing only: getting it down without looking like a silly, inexperienced fool.

It tasted a lot like how nail polish smells, terrible in the most aggressive of ways.

"It's better if you plug your nose," she said after I'd swallowed mine and finished an involuntary shoulder-shimmy. "That's what I do after the first wakes me up."

Warmth radiated from the bottom of my belly. A voice of false confidence screamed into the void of my mind. It begged me to take a couple more shots and ride the night out. Risk it all. Maybe even tell her.

When I reached for the bottle again, Kai grabbed my wrist and held it. "Ease into the night," she said. "Getting too drunk too fast isn't any fun. And the hangover's even worse."

I went against my body's desires and nodded back at her. We situated ourselves in the rocky sand and stared up at the stars, our bodies mere millimeters away from each other as the cheap vodka swirled in the pits of our stomachs.

The entire world spun slowly around the clearing, picking up speed with every rotation.

"I've never felt anything like this before," I muttered. "My legs are freezing, but my chest is on fire. It's amazing."

Kai laughed, wriggling herself closer. Our ribs pressed against each other, yet we kept staring up at the stars and neither of us addressed it. "You haven't drank much before, have you?"

Moments prior, I would have made up some elaborate story or lie to save face, but I couldn't, not anymore. "Nope, not much."

"So that's why you got all weird when I pulled the bottle out," she said. "It all makes sense now."

"What does?"

"Why you were uncomfortable," she explained. "I wouldn't have pressured you into taking a shot if I knew."

I shrugged. "Don't worry about it. Going off to college without getting drunk wouldn't have been the best idea."

"Are you sure?"

"Absolutely," I replied. "This is already so much better than anything else I would have done tonight."

"Alright, you sold me. Time for another round."

Laughing, I struggled to push myself up. My body ebbed and

flowed with the world around us as she poured two more heavy-handed shots into our plastic cups. "On three?" I suggested as she handed me mine.

Kai smiled, nodded, and held her cup up, clinking it softly into mine. "To you," she said. "And making it as a journalist on the other side of the lake."

Her words doubled the feeling the vodka had brought, combining to fill my belly with warmth to capacity. We showed the bottoms of our cups to the moonlight.

The second swallow didn't burn nearly as bad as the first had, though its effects came twice as quick. I closed my eyes and swallowed once more. When we set them back down on the sand they were mostly empty, hearts artificially full, and the world was warm and spinning and beautiful.

"Do you think about him during nights like these?" I asked after a few minutes had passed. I knew it wasn't the best or most appropriate thing to ask her, but the vodka brewing in my stomach convinced me not to care. "You know, the rock star you dated in high school—Brett."

"Sometimes, but not tonight. Not recently."

I smiled and wiggled closer to her. The rocks dug against me through the sand, but I could hardly feel them. "What do you think about when you do think about him? Is it just reminiscing on old memories or something else?"

"That, and what we could've been. Sometimes I wonder if he ever loved me at all, if he even cared."

"How could he not? You're great."

Kai traced her fingertip over the back of my hand as she worked back toward the bottle. When she reached it, she grabbed it by the top and turned it upside down, drinking the pungent liquid straight without bothering to pour it into her cup.

"I appreciate you saying that," she said after putting the bottle back down between us. "But you have no idea what you're talking about. You can't."

"Why not?"

"You've never met him before."

"Still. I've got a feeling that I'm right."

"You barely even know me."

What she said was right, of course—I didn't know much about her at all, only that I was intrigued and desired more—yet I couldn't help but feel certain I was right. She just didn't strike me as somebody who could enter your life and leave forgotten or un-loved. The math didn't add up.

"I think about mine too. All the time. Sometimes it feels like I'll never be able to get her out of my mind."

"Trust me." Kai snorted. "I know."

"Right," I said, holding my hands up in mock defeat. "Sorry about that. Even when I'm happy or preoccupied or even with someone else she's always there, always lingering."

"Was she your first love?"

"More than that. My first girlfriend, my *only* girlfriend."

"Tell me about her then," she instructed. "I'm convinced that'll help. And if not, take another shot, and another and another until you feel better."

"Now that's hard logic to refute," I said, pushing my hands against the flattened rock we sat upon. It had cooled considerably since the sun had gone down.

Fog burned off the lake. I took another swig of vodka and began telling Kai the story of Tory and how we came to be an item. It billowed up toward the heavens as we reached the beaut-iful crescendo of a high school romance gone terribly wrong.

I was far too drunk to omit any of the embarrassing details. Once I started talking, I couldn't stop. It all came out raw and un-inhibited, even the Red Graduation. I pushed it all to the forefront and told her exactly how it was on no uncertain terms.

"That's so cruel," she said once I had finished. "I can't believe somebody would do something like that after being together for so long. You deserve so much better."

"Don't we all. But that's just how life goes, I guess."

"What do you mean?"

"It's unfair," I replied. "Stacked against us all. I deserved better than what Tory did to me, just like you deserved better than getting left in LA, yet they both happened anyway. Life doesn't care about individual people. It just unfolds. And we react."

"Quite the drunken nihilist, I see."

I gripped the bottle and took another swig, much heavier than the last two combined. "The truth is all we've got."

"What do you think's the solution?"

"See, that's the problem. There isn't one."

Kai sighed and moved closer to me as I struggled with the bottle in my hand. "Let me help you with that," she said, before grabbing it and taking another drink herself.

When she sat it down, a silence came over the clearing. Chirping birds and the distant sound of crashing waves were all that could be heard. Elwood Grove, as the creator intended.

Six inches slowly became two, and then, before I could even think about reacting, those two inches were reduced to zero and I found myself wrapped completely in her foreign arms, kissing somebody not named Tory for the first time in my life and loving every second of it.

She worked an arm slowly up my back before wrapping it around my neck, clinching me tight as she pulled herself against me. Chest to chest. Our kiss deepened. Sloppy and inexperienced in one way, perfectly measured in another. Her knee dug into the side of my hip as she swung her legs around to climb onto my lap.

Passion swelled through her fingers. They pushed past my tangled hair, contrasting against the night. Suddenly, it wasn't so cold anymore. The heat was consuming. Everything felt right—*she* felt right. I would have done anything to bottle the moment and preserve it forever.

"I want you," she whispered into my ear, panting heavily into my neck. "I need you right now."

Her words burned new, previously unknown synapses into my brain and made the tiny hairs on the back of my neck and arms stand straight up. I wanted her more than words could ever articulate. Yet I also knew, deep inside, that I couldn't go forward.

I knew that I couldn't grab her and do what we both wanted, what we both craved. It was impossible. No matter what I did, my body wouldn't allow it. I was frozen. And the worst part was that she would never know why. She would never understand.

"W-wait," I said, trembling as she worked her tongue up and down my neck, panting as she did. "Hold on—*stop!*"

"What's wrong?" Kai asked. She shifted her weight back and grinded into my lap some more. "Doesn't it feel good?"

"I'm sorry," I stammered. The world spun and twisted, turning as it constricted around me. It made less and less sense with each rotation. I was drunk and full of regret. "I'm sorry, but I can't do this. We can't do this. Not right now."

Kai pushed herself from my lap and struggled to find her footing on the dark, moonlit sand. Most of the fog had risen from the lake. It covered the moon almost entirely, turning everything black. We were all invisible.

"It's not you," I began. "It's—"

"Don't do that," she interrupted. "You don't have to do that, not with me. I know when I'm wanted and when I'm not."

"It's not that. I've just never done this before."

"You're a virgin?"

I nodded. It wasn't a lie.

"Oh," she said, suddenly returning to her former self. "Don't worry about that. I don't care. It doesn't bother me."

"Maybe not you, but it does me."

She grabbed me by the shoulders and tried kissing me again, but I pulled away. Our eyes locked. The moment intensified.

"Relax," she whispered. Her voice was calm and direct. "Just relax and let me lead. I'll show you the way."

"You don't understand," I said, pushing her off again. "I can't do this. Not right now."

"When can you?"

"Maybe not ever."

"What's going on?"

But I couldn't answer, not honestly. So I sighed and told her I was sorry again.

Then I walked away, leaving her alone and confused.

9

When I told Finley what happened with Kai, I glossed over many of the more troubling details. I told him how beautiful the night had been, but left out how I'd ruined it all. Not a singular word was spoken about how the night had ended with me drunk and alone, shivering in an empty parking lot without a wink of sleep.

"How are things with Mathew?" I asked before he could press for more details about my story. "Seen much of him lately?"

"The party was the best I've ever been to," he said. His voice roared with pride. "And then we went out for breakfast just the two of us."

"See. I told you."

"I just might end the summer with a bid."

"More than that."

"Shut up," he said, but smiled.

We coasted off the highway onto one of the poorly paved side roads leading to the beach. Sand, rain, and drunk teenagers made it more trouble than it was worth for the city to properly maintain them, so local lawmakers made the executive decision to let the potholes stay. Thick weeds grew between the cracks, while they rationalized that the lake was enough of a draw to keep the tourist revenue coming in. The issue was that they were right.

"Do you think it'll be awkward?"

"Why would it?"

"I can't think of any place I belong less than a beach party with a bunch of frat boys."

"A beach *darty* with a bunch of frat boys," Finley corrected.

"My point exactly. I don't even know what it's called."

"You should invite Kai—"

"She's busy."

"Oh, well, looks like it'll just be us then, a throwback to how things used to be."

"Plus a bunch of frat boys I've never met."

"It'll get you ready for next fall when you come visit me at IU. Come on, you know you're at least a little excited."

"Nothing will get me ready for that."

My mind began to descend as we crossed the next half-mile of road. I lingered on what he'd said. Everything would be so different in the fall. Finley would be holed up in some frat house in Bloomington, drinking and partying himself into oblivion, while I struggled my way around Evanston chasing a dream.

Our lives would become unrecognizable to the other, and it seemed like there was no feasible, realistic way that we would make it through. But I kept my mouth shut and didn't vocalize any of my doubts. There were much more important matters at stake.

Sand burned the bottoms of my feet as we walked toward Stop 2 and the promise of Mathew's band of fraternity brothers. Teen-agers who were obviously still in high school played beer pong and shouted incoherently at us. Our feet never stopped moving.

"I think that's them," Finley mumbled once we'd reached the base of the biggest dune. He pointed up toward a crowd of seven or eight guys. They were all shirtless and wearing extra short swim trunks and looked largely the same.

"Which one is he?"

"Right over there. Do you see him?"

I squinted up the dune, but couldn't distinguish Mathew from the rest of the cluster. We were headed up to them regardless, so I shrugged and offered a noncommittal grunt.

The group of boys became clearer the further we climbed up the dune. Finley's eyes hadn't deceived him. Mathew was there, standing proud in the center of them all. "There you are," he said once he caught sight of us. He grabbed Finley by the waist and pulled him into a hug. "I'm glad you came."

They lingered in each other's arms for a while before finally breaking free. I was left alone, markedly unhugged with my arm outstretched in anticipation of a handshake that never came. The rest of the brothers looked at me with standoffish eyes, like I was a foreign entity they weren't yet accustomed to.

I remained on the outskirts of their circle as Finley continued to talk to Mathew and the other brothers returned to their games of flippy cup and beer pong. They all looked so happy, I thought. Happy and together. I couldn't help but feel a little jealous. Maybe Finley had been onto something all along.

● ● ●

The circle of frat boys waxed and waned throughout the next few hours. Half the brothers left around noon to "go find some girls" and were quickly replaced by another line of obedient drinking soldiers with a penchant for Mathew and doing whatever he said.

None of them talked to me much—usually just a quick hello followed by simple pleasantries before moving on—yet they seemed to take an early liking to Finley. He ingratiated himself effortlessly into the intimate folds of their social group. It was like he'd known them his whole life, like they were the best of friends.

"I'm going for a walk," I said, whispering into his ear after forty-five minutes of acting like I was happy and content laying out in the sun while the rest of them drank and partied. "Text me if you need anything."

"You're leaving?" he questioned. His eyes looked genuinely surprised. "Why would you want to do that? The party's just getting started."

"It's too loud. I need to think."

He threw a clumsy arm over my shoulder, nearly knocking us both down in the process. "Think about what?" he asked. "Is something going on?"

"Nothing. Just college stuff."

"Want me to come with?"

"Of course not. You're like a kid in a candy shop right now. I couldn't drag you away from this even if I wanted to."

"I can leave if you need me to," he insisted.

"Stay here and have some fun. Enjoy your time with Mathew. I'd rather be alone right now anyway. It's best for both of us."

"You sure?'

"Absolutely."

It only took me walking a few steps away for the circle to tighten and erase my existence entirely. We had so many differences already, leaving for separate colleges would only make them more pronounced. I glanced back and saw Finley taking the first shot in a new game of beer pong. His eyes never found me.

Doubts of our future and what our relationship would one day become carried me through the first few dunes. They were filled with people I had graduated with, the same ones who had watched Tory humiliate me in front of the entire auditorium and laughed and laughed as they recorded videos that filled my Snapchat feed. None of them spoke to me as I walked past.

I became so wrapped up in avoiding their eyes that I didn't notice my old AP Chemistry lab partner unfolding a beer pong table in front of a crowd of our old classmates. I walked straight into his back like I had the banner at gradation.

"Sorry," I mumbled, eyes locked on the sand. "Didn't see you there. My bad."

He grunted something unintelligible in response. I nodded and jogged away in the opposite direction. Small talk would inevitably follow if I lingered too long. So I jogged the next two hundred yards.

When I looked up she was there.

Tory stood prominently in front of a large gathering of our

former friends, wearing the crimson one-piece she'd bought on our trip to Myrtle Beach over Spring Break.

She looked beautiful, alluring in the worst of ways. We locked eyes. My heart collapsed as she approached. "We need to talk. Do you know anywhere private that we can go?"

"You made it pretty clear how you felt at graduation. What else is there to talk about?"

"Don't be like that, Lou. Let's just go somewhere and talk. We can't stay like this forever. Come on. You know we need it."

I wanted to laugh in her face and send her back to our old friends with tears in her eyes, but couldn't and knew I never would. My chest crooned with the desire to follow her to the edge of the world. Or maybe it was longing, I couldn't tell. Either way, I submitted, and told her to follow me.

She asked me how much further we had several times as we crossed the dunes headed to Elwood Grove. This continued throughout our entire ascent to the clearing. "We're almost there," I muttered under my breath.

Gusts of cool summertime air blew off the lake. It contrasted nicely with the burning sand under our feet as we took our first step out onto the clearing. Tory took a few steps in front of me and looked around. Her body language was the exact opposite of how mine had been. I looked over, thoroughly confused, and ushered her forward so she could get a better look.

"Are we there yet? Is this it?"

"Isn't it beautiful?"

"It's private. Now can we talk?"

Her voice sounded utterly nonplussed. And suddenly, in that moment, I realized that I'd made a huge mistake bringing her there. Kai never should have trusted me. She had given me something sacred, something personal to her that hardly anybody else knew about, and I'd repaid her by telling my ex and bringing her in on everything we shared.

"Yeah," I replied, trying my best to quell my free-falling inner monologue. My mistake had already been made. All I could do was make the best of it. "Do you like it?"

"It's alright."

"Just alright?"

"How come you never took me up here while we were together? Why'd you keep it a secret all those years."

"I didn't know about it back then."

"Who took you up here?"

"Nobody," I lied. "I found it with Finley a few days ago. We got bored hanging out at Stop 2 all day, so we decided to start exploring the Grove and ended up here."

"So you guys are still hanging out."

"He's been my best friend since elementary."

"I always thought you'd eventually outgrow him," Tory said with a shrug. "You're moving to the big city, and all he cares about is chasing frat boys."

"Evanston," I corrected. "And who cares that we're different? It's never mattered before. Why would it now?"

"People drift away when they stop making sense."

She always knew how to pinpoint my unspoken insecurities and twist the knife. "So that's what we're calling it now."

"Don't oversimplify what happened," Tory said. Her upper lip twitched before dying and going stoic.

"You broke up with me in an auditorium full of our closest friends," I replied. "That's horrible, but not exactly complicated."

"We needed a clean break."

"Maybe so, but you didn't have to do it like you did, in front of everybody. You didn't have to hurt me like that."

"I—"

"No. You chose to."

10

Rays of early-morning sun burned petulantly through my blinds. They backlit my eyelids, turning the cold darkness pale orange. I slowly woke and came to. With consciousness came doubt, coupled with regret. Morning crust was still baked into my eyes, but there was only one thing on my mind. One question repeating endlessly, demanding to be answered.

Why did I bring her to the clearing?

Sighing, I pulled myself out of bed and stumbled toward the pantry. When I reached it, I pulled open the door and found myself facing an old bottle of vodka head on. It didn't look much different than the one Kai had back at the beach.

Memories of her and the feelings of our night together drew me in. They were intoxicating. So I pulled the bottle out, twisted off its cap, and showed the bottom to the ceiling and took a deep, burning swallow. I repeated this process twice in quick succession.

My bed felt a lot more comfortable when I returned to it after my early-morning shots. I closed my eyes and released a deep, un-inhibited sigh. A few hours sleep would do me good, I thought hopefully. The only problem was that I wasn't alone.

The tiny green orbs were back, staring at me in the dark abyss of my brain. They hovered just on the edge of view, lingering insistently as they taunted my every thought.

Opening my eyes was the only way to rid myself of them, but as soon as I closed them they were back and closer and worse than before. This effect compounded with every blink. Sweat began to puddle on my forehead.

Gasping, I opened my eyes, rolled over, and fumbled on the bedside table for my cell phone. When I found it, I dove into my contact list and found Kai's name, then gave her a call.

"What do you want?" she snapped, interrupting the fourth ring midway through. "Let me guess, you want to talk about what happened at the beach?"

"Yes, I—"

"Well I don't want to," she interrupted. There was another voice talking on Kai's side of the phone call, but it wasn't loud or clear enough for me to understand what they were saying.

"Wh-What are you doing?"

"What do you want?" she asked again. Her voice was flat and direct, unbothered.

"I need to see you again."

She laughed. "Why would you want to see me again? You made it pretty clear you didn't want anything to do with me."

"You don't understand," I replied. "I can't stop thinking about you and how I ruined something that could've been special before it even began."

"I'm not going to argue with you there."

"Exactly. That's why we need to talk."

"Say what you have to say. Whatever it is, you can do it over the phone. Spit it out so we can get this conversation over with."

It was my turn to laugh. "No way. Three shots aren't nearly enough for that."

"Three shots?" she questioned. I could tell from her voice that she was perking up on the other side of the line, intrigued. "Why are you taking shots this early in the morning when you don't even drink? What's going on over there?"

"I'm just working through some things."

"Are you okay?"

"I'm sad and I need to talk to you. But other than that, yeah, I'm fine—never been better."

"Fine," she sighed. "Text me your location. Looks like you're getting what you wanted. I'm coming over after all."

I almost dropped my phone in the excitement that followed. She was coming over. She was really, actually coming over. Maybe there was hope for us yet.

"Are you sure?" I asked. I don't want to force you into doing something you—"

"Shut up and send me the location."

I opened my mouth to say something back—an apology, perhaps; or even better, an explanation—but decided against it and kept my lips together. She was coming over, and that was all that mattered. I couldn't ruin the second chance that had fallen into my hands. So I just said okay.

After hanging up the phone I stood up from my bed and looked into the vertical mirror hanging at its foot. Two heavy bags stared back. My hair jutted out in every direction. I looked terrible. A sad, desperate excuse of a man. I stood upI had to go to the bathroom and make myself presentable. The world continued spinning. It always would. Kai was on her way.

Physically making it there proved much harder than I'd imagined. The hardwood floor connecting my bedroom to the hallway and the rest of the house liquefied as I stepped onto it. I steadied myself with a hand against the wall until I reached the sink in the bathroom and turned it on.

Ice water splashed against my face, but didn't do much. The vodka had fully taken over. Its burning tendrils wrapped tightly around my neck, strangling me from the inside out. There would be no breaking free, only riding it out. But Kai was coming.

● ● ●

I heard her arrive long before I saw her car out the window. Tires crunching into gravel, a struggling engine sputtering, a slamming door, then footsteps that got louder and louder until they suddenly stopped. A loud knocking sound replaced them and reverberated through the entire house. I stood up from the couch.

The ground shook even worse than it had before when I took my first step. I had forgotten how drunk I truly was in the time that had passed since sitting down. Nothing made that more apparent than trying to walk. Still, I just about managed to slide the deadbolt loose and open the door without stumbling or falling over myself.

And there she was.

No more than three or four inches and a small plastic piece of trim separated us. She looked as beautiful as ever. Beautiful with her guard up, fortified to the best of her ability. I'd lost her trust even quicker than I'd gained it.

"You look gre—"

"No," she interrupted. "We're not doing that. That's not why I'm here. Not after last night Just tell me what's going on and why you're drinking so I can leave."

"I'm so sorry." I looked pathetic, but it was true.

"Forget it," she said quickly. I could tell from her voice that she was making an honest effort to act like she didn't care. "We were both drunk. I made a mistake. Move on."

"You didn't make a mistake—"

"How much have you had to drink?"

"Nothing since we got off the phone."

"So just the three shots you already told me about?"

I nodded, and as I did, I noticed the muscles connecting her neck and shoulders relax. She didn't have to say that she cared. It was obvious.

"Why did you leave?" she asked after a while, voice hardly a whisper. "Everything felt like it was going so well, then all the sudden it wasn't anymore. What happened?"

"I guess it was just too much too fast," I said, despite knowing full well that it was a lie. "I wasn't ready."

"I shouldn't have pressured you."

"No—"

"I'm sorry." All the anger and embarrassment had left her voice. We locked eyes and stared, hard.

"You shouldn't be the one apologizing."

"Of course I should. I made you uncomfortable."

"No. You don't understand."

"Then explain it to me. Make me understand."

"How long do you have?"

She took a step inside and sat down on the edge of the couch. We were close, but she remained standoffish. "However long it takes. I'll stay right where I'm at until I understand whatever it is that I don't right now."

I sighed and followed her lead, situating myself a few feet away from her on the opposite side of the couch. It was hard enough to keep my tears contained sober. Drunk, I was hopeless. I knew where our conversation was headed and didn't know if I'd be able to stop it. I buried my face into the palms of my hands. An uncontrollable wave of tears coated the carpet below.

"Truth is I was scared," I said, speaking at last, though I still couldn't bring myself to meet her eyes. "Scared that if you knew the truth you wouldn't want anything to do with me."

"Why would I care about you being a virgin?" she asked. "It's not like we're forty-five or something. There's nothing for you to be embarrassed about."

"You don't—"

"Stop telling me that I don't understand."

"Please," I whispered. "Listen to what I'm saying, please. Hear me out before you jump to any conclusions. Everything will make sense when I'm done. Trust me."

"Fine, go on. I'll just sit over here and listen."

"Thank you." I stared down at the floor between the cracks of my hands. "Being with you is all I want. It's all I wanted then, and it's all I want now."

The words I wanted to say stood prominently in my mind, flashing against the tiny green orbs, yet I couldn't bring myself to force them out. "Never mind," I finally managed. "Forget about this. All of it. I'm still not ready."

She pushed herself off the couch with a loud huff and shook her head, then told me that she was leaving and we were done for good. "I can't take this anymore. You're so confusing."

My muscles tightened. I was losing her for good. I clasped my eyes shut, and fought to hold the tears back, but couldn't. They fell everywhere without shame. My fight was over.

"What's wrong?" said Kai from above. Her hand rubbed tight circles into my shoulder. "You're shaking. What's going on?"

"No," I replied quickly, then shook my head and stopped myself. "I mean nothing—I'm fine."

She sat down on the couch, much closer to me than she had before. Her anger had disappeared almost entirely, replaced by something worse—pity.

"You can tell me. Whatever it is."

I sighed again, forcing my eyes open as I continued to stare at the carpet between my feet. "A lot of stuff happened to me. It was a long time ago. I was young, a little kid."

The circles on my back slowed. She wrapped an arm around my waist, pulled me close, and held me there without saying a word. I could feel her breath on my neck.

"I didn't want him too," I continued, digging the tips of my fingernails into the leather of the couch with all the strength I could manage. "I told him to stop so many times, honest, but he just wouldn't. He wouldn't listen no matter I did. He wouldn't stop no matter what I said."

She squeezed me tighter so that our bodies were pressed flush against each other. She held me to make sure that I knew she was there, and that she wasn't going to leave.

"He did whatever he wanted. He wouldn't stop."

"It's not your fault," she whispered. "Whatever happened to you back then, it's not your fault. None of it was."

Tears began to fall once more; thick and fast, in hopeless flutters. There was no point trying to conceal them. Even if she didn't know everything, she certainly knew enough to know that they were coming and inevitable. The seal had been broken; the tap was leaking without a plumber in sight.

"That's why I want to be a journalist."

Kai's head swung to face me. "What did you just say?"

"That's why I want to be a journalist."

"I don't understand."

I sighed and sat up, pivoting my body to face her directly. We locked eyes and I shook, but didn't waver. "Everything that happened to me back then, *that's* why I want to be a journalist."

The wrinkles on her forehead sunk deeper into the slightly red canvas of her skin. "I'm still struggling to understand how the two are related."

"My story is all I've got. He took everything else."

She looked at me with intent eyes, but kept her lips pressed firmly together. She was far too caught up with the anticipation of what I'd say next to speak herself.

"It's all about the story," I explained. "About representation, you know—the truth. Back when I was a little kid and the wounds were still fresh and new and foreign I looked everywhere I could for somebody like me. All I wanted was to find a story that even somewhat resembled my own.

"Anything would have been enough. A book, movie—hell, even an article would've done it. But there was nothing. I stumbled on a few things targeted at little girls who had gone through similar things, but there was nothing for us boys.

"We were less than zero, alone. Lost boys in every sense of the word. The more I read, the more I realized it was true. That's when I realized something had to change. And if nobody was willing to do it, then I decided I would."

Kai wrapped her other arm around my waist again and pulled me closer to her, squeezing me tight. "So it's like therapy, sort of? Writing everything thing down to process."

"No," I replied. My eyes were shut. Everything was dark except for the two green orbs. They remained, still hovering as always. "Not even a little bit. The scars he left are permanent.

Writing only makes it worse. They'll never go away, not entirely."
     "Why keep doing it then, if it doesn't help at all?"
     "For the next me."
     "The next one?"
     I nodded.
     She reached over to squeeze my hand.
     "There will always be another."

11

Kai lingered on my mind long after she left. I'd gone against thirteen years intuition and done the one thing I promised myself I never would. And my body shook because of it, trembling at the mere thought of her reaction after a night in retrospect. Everything had been perfect, but would it last? Or would it change? There was no way to know. The power rested in her hands.

The rational part of my brain told me that I was overreacting and being stupid obsessing over it. Brett had left her high and dry in the outskirts of Los Angeles and she'd done nothing in retaliation. So why would she go out of her way to hurt me when I'd done nothing wrong? Still, my nerves were palpable and only growing. They wouldn't go away.

I lost the rest of the evening to an intensely hyperbolic, unrealistic doomsday-fiction about how Kai would run all around Long Beach telling anybody who would listen what happened to me, and then they would all stand around in a big circle and laugh at my expense like they had at graduation.

"Are you feeling alright?" Mom asked seconds after I stepped into the kitchen and grabbed a mug from the cupboard. She lingered over my shoulder and filled the mug with coffee straight from the pot. Steam wafted up, fogging my glasses.

I inhaled and let the coffee's bitter scent fill my nostrils. It was almost comforting. "Just a little tired, that's all."

"Rough day yesterday?"

"Same as any other."

She sighed and sat down at the table with heaping plates of eggs and hash browns. Steam billowed off the top. They were piping hot, straight from the pan. "What'd you do?"

"Nothing much. Just went to the beach with Finley."

"What's with the sudden interest in the beach this summer?" she asked. "You never used to go. Sounds like there's something going on there I don't know about."

"Nope," I lied. "Nothing at all. There's just nothing better to do in Long Beach. The beach is the best thing we've got."

She smiled cheekily. "You could always stay home and hang out with your mommy."

"I would have yesterday, but you left before I got up."

"Yesterday was an exception." Mom sighed and shook her head. "Your uncle needed my help. I couldn't leave him high and dry, not after everything he's done for us."

"Everything he's done for us," I scoffed.

"What's that about?" she questioned. "He's done so much for this family. He's been the perfect role model for you."

I looked away and forced a curt nod. There was no way I would be able to tell her without collapsing from the anxiety. Telling Kai had almost done me in, and she was nearly a stranger.

She relaxed into a smile and took a bite from her plate. "Want to get ice cream later? We could go to that place by the beach. Remember Paddy's? You used to love going there as a kid."

"Can't," I replied. A groan of faux-disappointment escaped my lips. "I already told Finley I'd meet him at Stop 2."

"How's he been?" Mom asked, sighing.

"Crazy about his new guy."

Her eyes perked up. "Anything serious?"

"I don't know, it's too early to tell. He seems to like him a lot, though. A lot more than any other guy he's been with. Something about this one feels different."

"Forget about the ice cream then," she said, sounding almost giddy as she spoke. "That can wait. Anything to get that boy to settle down is fine by me."

"IU's not exactly the best place for that."

"You're probably right, but it can't hurt to try. Either way, have fun. And stay safe. Dinner should be ready by the time you get home."

My head hung low on my walk out of the kitchen, and remained that way until I was out the door. The shame ate away at me. I was making things up about my best friend to cover the truth. What kind of son did that make me? What type of man?

Regardless of its negative ramifications, lying was a necessary evil in the grand scheme of things. It was justified by the end of summer, I thought as I climbed into my car and pulled out of the driveway. The logic wasn't great, but it was enough.

I pushed down on the gas pedal and merged onto the highway headed downtown. If everything worked out it would all be worth it, that much I knew for sure.

The traffic was light—the commuter rush heading into Chicago had long passed—and I reached her neighborhood much quicker than I'd anticipated. Two red lights turned green, I stepped on the gas, and before I knew it, I was there.

All the houses in her cul-de-sac were near-exact replicas. The only difference being that they were painted in slightly different colors, though they were all complimentary and from the same palate.

I took five laps around the entrance before finding the courage to pull in and park by the curb. My car idled softly as I pushed out a text through fidgeting fingers. *Look outside. I've got a surprise for you.*

My foot tapped up and down after I hit send, dancing an anxious ditty in anticipation of her response. I hadn't felt such intense nerves since my first date with Tory. I'd puked three times in the bathroom of the Peter Cat that day, and we were just meeting up after school to do some homework. Thankfully, my stomach was empty.

Before coming outside, Kai poked her head through the gap in her living room curtains. Her eyes danced around the neighborhood before landing on me and my car and lingering there. When we locked eyes everything was understood; she smiled. The front door soon swung open and she ran out in my direction. It was still swinging on its hinges when she reached the car.

"What are you doing here?"

"I've got a surprise for you. Get in the car."

"Another surprise?" she asked. Her smile grew as she circled the car and dove into the seat next to me. "Here's to hoping it's better than the last."

"No more talking about our exes."

"But that was my favorite part."

We pulled away from the curb, the car rumbled, and we began heading downtown.

"Looks like you'll have to live without it."

I pushed down on the gas pedal and accelerated down the street. Sitting next to her in silence and being comfortable with it felt wonderful. It was better than talking to anybody else.

There was something beautiful about the unspoken moment, but I couldn't maintain it as we rolled to a slow stop at the intersection of Cleveland and Wabash. "You're all I've been able to think about lately," I said.

She rested her hand on my thigh and rubbed small, methodic circles into it as I drove through the UAD and pulled into the parking lot of Kyoto Sushi. "Do you think anything's changed?"

I turned the car off. My fingers remained wrapped around the wheel, white-knuckling as I asked her what she meant.

"Between us," she elaborated, making direct eye contact as she did. "Do you think anything's changed? You know, now that I know what happened."

My heart sank. Both of our doors remained firmly locked and shut as we descended into silence again at speed. We were locked in an airtight smother box. There was no place to run, much less to hide.

"What're you talking about? I still don't understand."

She let out a sigh, and with it, removed her hand from my leg. "Do you think you'd be able to move on now that you've told somebody? Did it make anything better?"

"I'm not over it, if that's what you're asking."

"No." She shook her head. "That's not what I meant."

"Then what *do* you mean?"

She buried her face into her palms. "You're really going to make me say it outright, aren't you?"

"Say what?"

"Do you think you can have sex?" she asked. "You know, now that you've told me."

Every word out of her mouth pushed the pit in my stomach deeper and deeper until it was ground into a microscopic powder between my feet. It had only taken one day to make the mistake that undid thirteen long years of work. Her expectations were way off, totally unreasonable. I glanced out the window and looked down the street. The restaurant was empty. We were alone.

"Probably not—well, I don't know really. Not right now at least, I don't think."

"You're so much more than whatever happened to you back then, Lou. Don't ever forget that."

"People love saying that. I'm unconvinced."

"Why not?"

"Life," I said. "Reality has taught me that it's simply not true. The truth is that I'm nothing more than what he did to me that day. Nothing less, but nothing more either."

"That's not true."

"Think about it. I only exist because of what happened that day. Without it, I'd be entirely different."

"You can't actually believe that."

"I wouldn't be the man I am today if it wasn't for him. Who knows how I would've turned out? Maybe better, but maybe worse too. Either way, I would be fundamentally different."

She grabbed my leg again and held on tightly. "No," she whispered, looking me straight in the eyes. "He didn't make you into the man you are today. You did."

I sighed and averted her gaze. The streets remained empty. We were still alone. "Oh, if only that were true. Everything would be so much simpler."

"He's not the one that got you writing—"

"I don't even write," I interjected. "All I do is think about it, and procrastinate. I haven't actually written any real, meaningful words in years. There's always something more pressing going on, always an excuse."

The circles stopped against my thigh again. Instead, she gave me a firm, concentrated squeeze. "Come here," she said, speaking into the space between us, tracing her finger up my thigh and body until her hand was tucked behind my head and we were kissing like we had at the clearing.

But the kiss was short-lived. I pushed her away before it could deepen. "He broke me that day," I went on. "And I've spent the last thirteen years lying to everybody and seeing him all the time. Birthdays, vacations—every family dinner. He's always there. He's always staring."

"But you're almost free," she argued. "Pretty soon you'll be moving to Chicago and never have to see him again."

"Running away and hiding on the other side of the lake isn't going to change the problem. It'll just move it."

"He didn't break you. Nobody can."

"I appreciate you saying that—really, I do—but I don't think that you're right. Sometimes the truth hurts and hits you hard because it's unfair and horrible. This is one of those times."

"You have to—"

"Can't we just go inside and talk about something else, *anything* else. This isn't what I had planned at all. Let's go eat and try to have a good time together, please."

Her eyes widened in fear as I gripped the door handle and

pulled it open. "I'm only trying to help," she said. "I don't want you to be uncomfortable."

"I know you don't," I said, speaking in a voice that was hardly audible. "That's why I'm not mad at you right now."

I held the door open and stared into her eyes until she broke and stepped through. Only a few weeks had passed since graduation, yet my life was indecipherable from what it had been.

A small, long-haired Japanese man who looked to be in his mid-thirties greeted us at the door and asked us if it would just be us two, or if we were waiting on any more people. When I spoke up and said no, he gave me a curt nod and led us to a table near the back of the dining room. It didn't have the best view, but it was tucked away and intimate enough that we could talk without fear of interruption or being overheard.

"I know you said you didn't want to keep talking about it, but I think I've got a way for you to get past what he did to you."

I sighed and stared down into the table separating us. "I seriously doubt that," I said. "But you're not going to let it go until I hear you out, aren't you?"

"It'll work. Trust me."

"Fine," I sighed. "What is it?"

"Tell the world your story."

"What did you just say?"

"I'm being serious," she continued. Her voice sounded much more indignant than anything I'd heard from her before, so I couldn't help but fall silent and hang onto the anticipation of whatever would come next. "Write your story exactly how it happened, write exactly what he did to you, and then send it out and publish it for the world to read."

"That's a terrible idea."

"Think about it. It's the only way."

"You think I can just publish something whenever I want to? Or that I'd even want to do that? It's not that easy, you know."

"It won't be easy at all," she replied. "In fact, it'll probably be the hardest thing you've ever done. But it'll be worth it."

"Yeah, and how's that? Fill me in."

"Think about the next you, the one that hasn't been born yet. This is the leap you were born to take. It only takes one yes."

Our waitress returned before I could respond, effectively salvaging our second first date. "Can I get you two started off with anything to drink?" she asked.

"Two waters."

"Anything else?"

"We need a few minutes," Kai said.

The waitress gave us a tight nod before walking away. Our table was silent within five steps. My eyes remained locked on the empty plates and chopsticks, but I could feel her eyes burning into the top of my head.

"Look," I said after a while. "I know that you think you're helping me right now, but this isn't. You're not. I can't just 'tell the world my story' or whatever else you've got in your head. That's not how journalism works.

"Hell, that's not how the *world* works. You don't get what you want just because you want it and try real hard. No, you need credibility first. And I don't have any, not yet at least. That's why I'm going to Northwestern in the fall."

Kai grabbed my hands and squeezed them until I looked up at her. "Forget all that. You don't need Northwestern, credibility, or anything else—"

"Let me guess. Everything I've ever needed is already tucked away somewhere inside of me. That's it, isn't it?"

"Sure," she scoffed. "Don't take me seriously."

"Fine, I'll play along. What should I do?"

"Sit down, write the article, and when you're done send it out to anybody and everybody you can until one of them says yes and agrees to publish it."

"And if none of them want it?"

"You fall back on the internet."

"Ah, the *internet*. Why didn't I think of that?"

"I'm serious," she replied. "It's the grand equalizer. If you write something good and true and it resonates with enough people, it'll eventually rise to the top. Somebody will find it and share it and somebody else will do the same. Your people will find you, Louie. I'm sure of it."

"That doesn't seem very realistic."

"The cycle of virality. We've seen it work a thousand times."

"Maybe, but not for me."

"Just do the work and they'll find you."

12

Cars were parked bumper to bumper all the way down Montgomery street, leading directly to Mathew's front door. And although our second first date hadn't gone as I'd hoped, Kai's unsolicited advice proved even further that she cared. Even after everything I'd said, she still cared.

That alone was more than enough to keep me going. So we all piled into my car and drove down to Mathew's beach house for one of his parties. I parked behind a Mercedes and gazed back at her. She smiled. All was well.

"Nobody mentioned that there would be so many people here," she said as we opened our doors and got out. "It looks like half the town showed up."

"I had no idea," Finley replied. "Mathew made it sound like an intimate little get-together on the phone."

I shook my head and slammed my door. We had wildly different definitions of the word intimate.

A visibly drunk frat boy sat on the bottom step of Mathew's front porch and whooped loudly in our direction. He raised a sloppy fist as we passed. "It's a good one in there," he stammered sloppily. "Party of the summer."

I nodded and forced a smile, then opened the unlocked front

door and stepped inside for the second time.

The luxury cars parked outside became drunken frat boys and trust fund babies as we crossed the threshold and entered the beach house. I looked to the left and saw a cluster of them belting out a synchronized song of hedonistic bliss as they grinded up against each other.

We shuffled straight into the heart of the chaos. A tall boy stumbled over and nearly knocked Finley off his feet, but he didn't react. He just laughed and we all kept moving.

Kai placed a hand on the small of my back and shepherded me toward the corner wall. We struggled through the crowd into the kitchen as some big hit pop ballad reverberated through the speakers. One of the brothers I'd met previously at the beach slammed into my side while shotgunning a beer. The surrounding crowd roared their approval. "What have we gotten ourselves in-to?" she whispered.

"Stop being so negative," Finley replied. "Mark my words. This will go down as the party of the summer."

"He's only saying that because Mathew's here."

"Oh, to be young and in love," Kai said. She laughed, elongating her voice as she wrapped an arm around Finley's shoulder and brought him into her.

Finley opened his mouth to respond, but no words came out. We rounded the corner, stepped properly into the kitchen, and found ourselves away from the heat of the party and mass of sweaty, grinding bodies. They were replaced by two short, sturdy-looking boys making out on the other side of the room. They looked in-credibly passionate, and more than a little bit drunk. When they broke apart time stopped moving.

It was Mathew.

The other boy's eyes widened. He looked over at us and saw six spheres of pure hatred staring back. He had no idea what was going on, of course, but took the hint quickly and disappeared into the living room without a word.

Mathew took a step forward and stood vulnerably in the center of the kitchen while we all looked on. Shaking at the wrist, he gripped the bottom of his shirt and tugged, hard. "I'm so——"

"Don't," Finley whispered, shaking himself. He cocked his head sideways and looked toward me and Kai. "I'm done. I can't deal with this," he continued. "Give me that bottle, Lou. I need to be drunk right now."

I looked back, confused, but said nothing.

"Give it to me. I need to get fucked up."

My eyes darted to Mathew. His forehead was littered with leathery lines of stress. He was clearly struggling to find the right words, but it was obvious he wanted to make things right and go back to how they were a few minutes ago. Nothing came.

Eventually, he shrugged his shoulders and let out a defeated sigh, then turned to walk away. "Take whatever you want," he muttered over his shoulder. "It's the least I can do. I'm sorry."

Kai grabbed a mostly full bottle of vodka from the countertop and followed Finley down an unknown hall. I glanced around before doing the same. It was much darker than the rest of the house. Nobody else was around. The only remaining hint that we were even at a party and not an empty house was the faint sound of music and trembling walls.

"Give me the bottle," Finley instructed.

I froze momentarily, but conceded quickly and passed it over. He unscrewed the top and turned it upside down, guzzling three or four heavy shots as it waterfalled into his open mouth.

We continued down the hallway, though it was a relatively aimless pursuit. None of us knew the house well enough to have any clue where we were headed, so we just kept our heads low and moved away from the music in whichever direction we could.

This eventually led us to a vacant spare bedroom. Finley stormed inside and collapsed onto the bed, while Kai turned the lights on and sat at the foot.

The unashamed wealth of the unused bedroom astounded me. It was massive, draped in decadence yet devoid of any life or character. Lifeless in every way, hollow. Stock photos of cities and skylines I'd never be able to afford lined the walls. I sighed and sat down next to Kai.

"I can't believe it," Finley muttered, falling backward to wallow in the linen. "They were all over each other—right in front of me. How could he?"

My eyes danced around the room desperate for something comforting to say, but there was nothing. The night had fallen apart with an exclamation. We were all doomed.

"It was like he didn't even care," he continued.

Kai sat down next to us. The bedframe creaked and the linen tensed, stretching into a moan beneath her weight. She placed a hand on the small of Finley's back and began working her fingers up and down his spine like she had mine before.

"Maybe he didn't know you guys were exclusive," she suggested. "Have you had the talk yet?"

Finley laughed maniacally and sat up on the edge of the bed. Vodka spilled from the corners of his mouth as he took an extra heavy double shot straight from the bottle, staining both our legs and the bedding too. It already reeked and we'd only been there a few minutes.

"Well, no. Not exactly."

"So not at all," she concluded.

"I thought it went without saying."

"Nothing goes without saying," she said, continuing to rub up and down his back. "People can't know how you feel if you never tell them."

"What am I supposed to do?"

"Lay down," she said. "Get some rest. Go find Mathew when you wake up. Tell him how you feel. Don't leave anything out."

"What about the other guy?"

"What about him? He didn't do anything wrong."

Finley closed his eyes and rolled over. His movements were wild and uncontrolled. He gripped the bottle again, but didn't raise it to his lips and didn't take a drink. Unsteady, trembling fingers wrapped around the label. He looked into our eyes.

"That guy back there has no idea who you are," Kai conjected. "He probably just met Mathew for the first time tonight. You know how it goes."

Finley clicked his tongue and swung the bottle upside down, taking another drink. "That's not very comforting."

"The truth rarely is. Now lay back down and get some sleep. Whatever you decide to do, it can wait until you're sober and fully aware. Let your mind clear itself before moving forward."

Finally, he broke, nodding obediently before guzzling down his next shot and falling back onto the bed. He looked up at the popcorn ceiling and smiled before closing his eyes.

"Now what do we do?" I asked after a minute or two had passed. "Should we leave? Staying here while he's asleep doesn't feel right. Intrusive, almost. I think we should go."

"He should be out for a few hours at least. Want to go get coffee or something? Maybe head to the beach?"

"Coffee sounds perfect right now."

"Perfect. Sit him up a bit and we'll go."

• • •

There seemed to be seven or eight new hipster or artisanal coffee joints popping up in the UAD every other weekend, yet there was only one that would do. The Peter Cat wasn't the nicest place on the block, but it was open from one in the afternoon to four in the morning. As such, it was the perfect place to take a girl after a party. Or any time, really. Most importantly, it was mine.

The old Frenchman was absent behind the counter once again as I opened the door. Between his unconventional hours and lackluster work ethic, I often wondered how he managed to keep the lights on. We walked in next to each other.

"Wow," she whispered, gazing up at the off-white fairy lights lazily strung up against the battered brick walls, dangling overhead. "It's a completely different place at night. So beautiful."

"That's what I've been trying to tell you," I replied. "Nothing beats the Peter Cat."

"Your clearing on the rocks."

I'd never thought of the Peter Cat that way, but I liked the way it sounded coming out of her mouth. A smile lingered on my face as we approached the counter. The old man's granddaughter did the same and asked what we wanted.

"Two coffees, please. Both decaf."

"Switching things up on me?" the girl asked. She put her book down and poured our coffee into plastic takeaway cups.

"It's too late for all that caffeine."

The girl nodded and swapped our coffees for a fistful of dollars. I smiled again, telling her to keep the change. Steam swirled off the top of our cups. I turned from the counter and led us back to the booth by the window. The street was quiet.

"Was it always Northwestern?" Kai asked.

I took my glasses off and tried wiping the fog from my lenses with the end of my shirt. "What do you mean?"

"Did you always want to go to Northwestern?" she elaborated. "Or were there others?"

Her question caught me off guard. I took a slow, deliberate drink from my coffee and thought it over. "Northwestern was always my first choice, but I applied to all the good schools."

"Did you get accepted anywhere else?"

"NYU and a bunch of safeties."

"You got into NYU?"

I nodded.

"Why didn't you go? I've always heard that New York City was the writing capital of the world. Seems like the perfect place for a journalist."

"A journalist, yeah, but not a young one."

"What makes you say that?"

"The market's way too saturated. There isn't any margin for error there. One mistake could cost you your career and get you blacklisted throughout the entire city."

"So you want to do some time in Chicago to hone your skills until you're ready to make the big leap into NYC?"

"Exactly. It's the perfect stepping stone."

Kai smiled and looked away. She stared wistfully out the window. "You've got your whole life figured out. It's almost like you've already lived it."

"There's so much I want to do and so little time to actually do it. I'm terrified that if I relax my twenties will slip away, and then my thirties will too. And one day I'll die, emptyhanded with nothing to show for all my years."

"Leaving was the best decision I ever made."

"Even after everything that happened?"

Still looking out the window, she let out a jaded sigh. *"Because* of everything that happened."

My eyes tightened. "Then why'd you come back?"

"It just felt right," she replied. "It was time."

A gust of quiet overtook the table as we both stared at out the window and thought over what the other had said. There weren't any cars driving by or people walking on the sidewalk. It was completely dark out. The city was ours.

"What's next?" I asked. "What's your plan?"

"My plan?" she returned. "I haven't had a plan in years. I don't even know what I'm doing tomorrow."

"Come on, there has to be something."

"I'm content with what I've got."

"Everybody's chasing something."

"Not me," she replied. "Life just kind of happens to me. Then I react, and that's it. The cycle repeats itself again and again."

"And that's enough for you?"

"Maybe not for tomorrow, but it is for now."

13

When I woke up the next morning there were four text messages waiting for me on my lock screen. Naturally, they were all from Finley. The first said he was alright, the second asked if he could come over, the third was about going to the beach, and then a decisive, conclusory fourth told me he was coming over regardless and was already on his way, so get up and get ready.

I sighed and sat up, leaning against the headboard as I wiped the morning crust out of my eyes before drafting my response. *I'm going to the beach anyway. Meet you there?*

His car horn screamed out less than five minutes after I had clicked send and rolled back over in bed. The noise made me jump off the bed and nearly run into the kitchen. Quickly, I filled my hands with sandwich supplies, stuffed them in my bookbag, and jogged out the door; he continued to honk the entire time.

"Sorry I didn't answer any of your texts last night," I said after we had driven for a few minutes. "I got caught up at the Peter Cat and didn't notice them."

"Don't worry about it. You're good. Everything worked out in the end."

I smiled and relaxed into the leather of my seat. "Oh yeah? What happened, then?" I asked. "Your texts took a sudden turn in the middle of the night. Did you take Kai's advice?"

He looked at me, confused.

"You don't remember. Did you talk to him?"

It didn't take any further prompting for Finley to dive headfirst into a lengthy story outlining how the previous night had gone. Some guy named Drew pulled him into a game of beer pong mere seconds after he'd woken up. Still half-asleep, he lost handily, then went outside. He found Mathew there, out on the porch alone, smoking a cigarette in deep contemplation.

"We talked the night away and ended up in his bedroom." he continued. "And everything was perfect. Things haven't felt this good between us since we first met."

My eyebrow raised. "Everything went perfect in his bedroom?" I asked. "Is that what you just said?"

"Not like that," he laughed. "We just sat by the window and watched the stars and talked until the sun came up."

"How do you feel now?"

"Alive, finally."

"So you're back together. That's perfect—congratulations!"

"Nope," he sighed. "That's not what I said at all."

He coasted to a stop near the parking lot off Stop 4 and shifted us into park. "Then what *did* you say?"

"He doesn't know if he has the time to have a boyfriend right now. He said he needs more time to think about it."

"And how does that make you feel?" I asked again. "It seems to me like you want a lot more than that."

Finley opened his door and stepped outside. I followed suit and did the same. I looked down the coast. Morning had already started to wane. People were everywhere.

"I'm not thrilled about it," he replied. "But what else am I supposed to do?"

"Tell him it's not good enough."

"I can't—"

"Make him make a choice."

Finley clicked his tongue and looked away, averting my gaze.

Unwavering, my eyes burned into the side of his skull. "What we have now is a lot better than nothing at all."

"Not if it's not what you want. Or if it isn't honest."

We walked down to the coastline with the intention of hugging the water until we reached the Grove. "I just can't lose him," Finley said softly. "That much is all I know. I can't lose him."

"You've got to stop putting him on such a pedestal," I replied. "That'll only lead to a broken heart."

Finley stopped abruptly and stood dead in his tracks. I stumbled ahead obliviously. "What's that supposed to mean?"

"Your relationship is incongruent."

"Incongruent?" he repeated, voice rising.

"Yeah. I don't think he's doing you right."

"Of course you would say that."

"I'm not going to apologize for not wanting to see my best friend get hurt by some frat boy he hardly even knows."

"Oh, well if *you* don't like him—"

"Don't be like this," I said, cutting him off. "You know I didn't mean it like that. That's not what this is."

"I should've known this is how you'd react."

I rolled my eyes and squinted, staring at him in the burning sunlight. "Fine, I'll bite. Go on. Tell me why."

"You don't want anything to detract from your spotlight," he said emphatically. "All you think about is yourself. You, and your self-imposed love triangle."

"What're you even talking about? I haven't mentioned Kai all day. And I'm certainly not in a love triangle."

"Your actions speak loud enough."

I scoffed in disbelief, but in the back of my mind the memory of taking Tory to the clearing played in a merciless loop. Nobody had forced me to bring her there. She hadn't even asked.

"When you're not talking about her, you're thinking about her, and when you're not thinking about her, you're moping around feeling sorry for yourself."

"I don't know what you're talking about."

"Look at today," he continued. "When I talked to you earlier this morning you said you had to go to the beach anyway. That was about her, wasn't it?"

"But I'm here with you no—"

"Only as an afterthought."

"So what?" I shot back. "Why does it matter that I'd be here anyway? There's nothing wrong with caring about both of you. It isn't illegal to care about two things at once."

"Nope, just selfish."

Before I could open my mouth and think of something to say, Finley turned his shoulder and was walking away. He glanced back at me after taking a few steps in the opposite direction. We locked eyes. He appeared devoid of any anger or contempt. Disappointment was all I saw.

I contemplated chasing after him, but there were too many people around, staring. And I didn't know what to say. A second coming of graduation was the last thing my life needed, so I kept my lips pressed tightly together and let him leave without a fight.

I was scared, frozen, terrified what each step meant and where it left us. Several people in the crowd snickered. My face burned.

I turned and walked away. Everything that could've gone wrong, had.

My bookbag bounced against the middle section of my back with every step I took, swinging side to side between my shoulder blades as I rounded the corners of the trail and navigated my way through the twisted, tangled overgrowth.

The sun burned unbearably hot overhead. My sweat nearly came to a boil as it leaked through the pores of my skin. I sighed, realizing that my kind-of-plan should have been put on the back-burner the moment Finley turned to walk away.

I should have dropped everything and chased after him, even if it meant canceling or rescheduling my planned surprise for Kai up on the clearing. But I couldn't bring myself to do it.

My feet kept moving forward, in the opposite direction as his. I kept walking away and doing exactly what he said I would. And my phone remained in my pocket, tucked away, forgotten.

Kai's moleskin bag was the first thing I saw when I stepped onto the clearing. It sat in the same place it had during our last night together, propped up behind the rock she liked to lean on.

I pushed away any lingering thoughts of Finley and the tumultuous state of our friendship and did my best to focus solely on the task at hand—the one I could still control—as I stepped into the middle of the clearing and crouched down.

The rocky sand cut up my knees and ankles as I examined my surroundings. There wasn't much to work with, but the rocks near the edge stood out. I got up, walked over to them, and brushed off the flattest rock I could find before unzipping my bookbag and dumping its contents—a towel, lunchmeat, condiments—onto my freshly-minted table.

Smiling to myself, I pulled my phone out. *Meet me at the clearing. I've got one last surprise for you.* Then I sat down on the rocky sand and looked out over the beach. A nervous, trembling sigh escaped my lips. The chips were set, all bets placed.

My phone buzzed. *Be there soon.*

• • •

It took her a little over hour to get to the clearing. When I finally heard her deft footsteps crunching against the leaves and dirt of the trail, my heart began to race and flutter and do all the cliches I previously thought impossible.

"What is all this?" she asked, gesturing toward the makeshift rock table I'd turned into our dining room for the evening. "You did this all for me?"

"It's not much, but it's the best view in Long Beach."

She rushed forward and enveloped me in a tight, consuming hug. "What are you talking about? It's perfect. I love it."

"I had to make things right after what happened."

Kai reached out and grabbed me by my wrists. She held them tight and steady, unwavering. "There's nothing to make right," she said firmly. "It was all a misunderstanding. We're good now."

"Still, you deserve something nice."

Her jacket rustled against my bare skin as we came together. The wind blew pieces of hair loose from her bun. Individual strands slapped my face. I took a collected breath inward and embraced the sweet scent of strawberry shampoo.

More than anything, I wanted to grab her face and kiss her exactly like we had before. But I couldn't find the nerve, and the moment passed. We separated and stared into each other's eyes. I had no idea what to do or how to react. "I hope you like sandwiches," I said stupidly.

Kai laughed. Her forehead crinkled and folded into itself as she looked me up and down curiously.

"Seriously," I went on. "It's all we've got."

She sat down on the sand next to our rock-table and began stacking turkey onto a slice of bread. Upon finishing, she lathered the remaining slice with mustard, then crammed the two of them together. "Who doesn't like sandwiches?"

I smiled and began building a sandwich of my own. It tasted aggressively average, but I hardly noticed. Looking across the rock and seeing Kai's smiling face staring back made all the struggle worth it, transforming what had started as a terrible day into a moment that would define my summer.

"This is the sweetest thing anyone's ever done for me," she said suddenly.

"You deserve so much more."

Her smile grew as she took another bite. "I'm here if you ever want to talk," she said. "Whenever you're ready, I'll be here."

My stomach dropped and rolled off the edge of the clearing, tumbling like a hopeless pebble to the beach below. "Thanks," I muttered, deadpan through clinched teeth.

"I'm serious," she persisted. "Stop thinking you're broken, because you're not. You're a great guy. One of the best I've met."

When I looked down at the table, I saw the forgotten remains of our sandwiches and everything good our date had just been. It had been going exactly as planned, better than imagined, yet she just wouldn't let it go. She pressed relentlessly. I stood up from the rock-table and sulked over to the edge of jagged rocks overlooking the clearing's edge.

The entirety of the beach and lake played out on the other side of the edge. Countless parties and the loudest music I'd ever heard. I looked out across the water and squinted. The pale outline of Chicago stared back, only just out of reach. A thick bead of sweat rolled over my upper lip before falling to the ground. I turned and faced Kai. We both stared.

The clearing was silent; the beach was still.

Kai made the first move. She wrapped one arm around my neck and placed the other palm on my cheek as the gap between us closed. Inches were slowly reduced to centimeters that quickly became nothing. Birds chirped; sand burned. Pop music continued to blare from the dunes beneath, backing it all. We were kissing and it all made sense.

Feeling her in my arms again made me not care so much that she kept bringing up the past and thinking up ways to fix me. Her intentions were good and that mattered so much more. She had given me another chance and I planned on taking it however it came. I closed my eyes. Our kiss deepened, and I succumbed to the moment entirely. In her arms, I was powerless.

The longer our kiss persisted, the closer we became. We melted down, then congealed back together before hardening as one. She jumped up with her arms around my neck and locked her legs around my back. I stumbled and fell softly into the sand. Her stomach heaved with laughter. Each inflection of her chest brought her hips up and down, grinding against mine.

She placed both her palms against my shoulder and pushed me deeper into the sand. It caught my exposed skin and burned. A sharp rock dug into my back. I felt none of it when she gyrated her hips. The world melted away. Nothing existed outside of her.

Her fingertips worked through my hair. I closed my eyes, entrusting my future to her for the second time. Whatever she said or did or desired would surely come to be. She held all the power.

There would be no other way. And I didn't mind it as long as she was on my lap and we were kissing.

But then, suddenly, she pushed back into my shoulders again, hard, and we broke apart. The air between us turned sharp. I snapped back into reality. The brunt of her weight pressed against my kneecaps. Her fingers lingered over the cool metal of my belt buckle. We locked eyes again, much more intense the second time around. She was panting. I understood.

I nodded. She nearly ripped off my pants.

Every grain of sand felt magnified against the backs of my legs and naked butt as she pulled my pants down to my ankles. They ground into me under the pressure of her climbing back onto my lap. Her shirt came off effortlessly, but my trembling hands struggled with the buttons of her shorts.

Anxiety compounded. I didn't know what to do with myself. Wind blew against our freshly naked bodies and sent goosebumps up and down. Seconds stretched to minutes, minutes to days.

She smiled and undid the buttons for me, but left her shorts up partially around her waist. I could see the edges of her panties. A bright yellow thong protruded, barely visible. My cheeks burned ten shades of red.

I'd never felt so vulnerable, yet I'd never felt so alive either. Her eyes staring down at me, her heaving chest; it was invigorating. A twig snapped somewhere in the forest behind us. I couldn't locate where the sound came from exactly, and I couldn't bring myself to care. She was consuming me. I was hooked. All that mattered was her increasingly naked body grinding into mine.

"Real classy," spoke a monotone voice from behind.

Kai, of course, had no idea who was talking. She leapt from my lap with a terrified shriek. Her naked body lingered half a foot above mine. It would've been a beautiful sight in differing circumstances. Shock and disbelief were plastered across her face, followed by so much confusion.

I scrambled to my feet and pulled my pants up, nearly falling over in the process. "Wh—Wh—What are you doing here?"

"I've been here every day," Tory replied. "Ever since you showed me. It reminds me of us. I didn't realize it was just the place you take all your girls."

"That's not—"

"Neither did I," Kai interjected. Her voice was cold, devoid of emotion, not unlike Finley's. She put her shirt back on and frantically redid the buttons.

"Who are you?" Tory asked.

Kai laughed. "I'm the one who showed him this spot," she replied. "Who are you?"

"Tory," I mumbled.

"Your *ex-girlfriend*, Tory?"

The hurt in her voice was palpable. It pounded into my skull, burrowing deep into my chest as it tore my heart to shreds. Kai was the perfect girl for me, the only person who had ever seen me for who I truly was and stayed. She hadn't judged me at all. And in response I'd betrayed her.

Tory took a step forward and stood directly between the two of us in the middle of the clearing. I shook my head, turned to Kai, and told her how sorry I was.

"What're you saying sorry to her for?" Tory asked. Her voice was sharp, a sucker punch to the gut. "You should be apologizing to *me*, not her."

"Why would I ever apologize to you?"

"For lying," she said. "And for bringing me here. You told me you found this place with Finley. But that was a lie too, wasn't it?"

"I—"

"Where does it end?"

"That's what you told her?"

I opened my mouth to respond, but all that came out was a series of incoherent stutters and nonsensical noises. There was no rational or reasonable way for me to explain myself. Words couldn't fix what I had done.

Kai looked at me, then down at the sand, sighing. "I can't believe you'd do this," she said. "I can't believe *I* almost did this."

No apology would ever be enough. I stared into her back as she walked away knowing that I'd lost her.

14

His green eyes returned in the night. I lost hours twisting and turn-ing, sleepless. They continued to taunt me well into the morning, corrupting the pale orange that usually colored my eyelids as it coaxed me awake. A yawn escaped my lips. I sat up and wiped the sleep from my eyes. There was nothing there.

The gravity of the previous day encumbered my mind. I struggled to fight against it. I had lost Tory against my will, then proceeded to lose my best friend and the most captivating girl I'd ever met trying to fill the void she'd left. None of it had worked. And I was left with nothing, much less than zero.

"Someone's up early," Mom said as I entered the kitchen. She was huddled over the stove, pinching small pieces of fresh basil into her morning tea. "Got anything going on today?"

I grabbed a can of iced coffee from the fridge, cracked it open, and took a sip. "Not really," I lied. "I think I'm just going to go to the beach to see what's up."

She snickered. "Shouldn't have asked."

"What's that supposed to mean?"

"You're always there. That's all."

"What's wrong with that?"

"Nothing," she replied. "It's just that you're leaving for school soon and you never spend time with me anymore. It seems like all you care about are your friends and that beach. I miss you."

My heart collapsed to the floor, accompanied by a groan that escaped my lips. No matter what I did, no matter how hard I tried, I just couldn't seem to get it right. Balancing my relationships and the people in my life felt an impossible task.

"I'd stay if I could."

"Then why don't you?"

"Because I already promised Finley that I'd meet him there."

Mom sighed into her cup of tea and slowly shook her head. It didn't feel good making a habit out of lying to her, but I couldn't think of a viable alternative. What other choice did I have?

"Any idea when you'll be back?"

"Dinnertime, hopefully."

• • •

Incongruent hypotheticals flashed through my mind as my car shook and struggled down the roads connecting my house and Finley's. On and on, the fragmented pictures repeated themselves in a brutal cycle that wouldn't end. I gripped the wheel and accelerated. My knuckles were pale by the time I reached his house.

I let the car idle at the curb and watched one of his neighbors meticulously pluck and prune his brilliant flock of petunias for at least five minutes, maybe even ten. With a false sense of gusto, I managed to turn the engine off and step out of the car. And the death march began, step after step until I reached his front door, then three hard, consecutive knocks.

The door nearly knocked me off the stoop when Finley shoved it open. "What are you doing here?" he asked sharply.

Regret began to set in, but I couldn't turn back. Forward was the only way. "Look," I began. "I know I haven't been a very good friend late—"

Finley snorted. "You can say that again."

I sighed, shaking my head. He was right and we both knew it. Arguing would only make things worse. It would rip the few remaining threads between us apart and that would be that. Our friendship would sing a whimpering swan song, then die an unremarkable death.

"I'm sorry."

"That's it? That's all you've got to say?"

"It's not much, but it's the truth."

He looked me over contemptuously, scowling up and down before pushing the door back open. Rooted to the center of the doorframe, he didn't move an inch.

"We can't let something petty like this get between us. I'm sorry, Finley, I really am. Please, let's talk it out."

"That's what we're doing right now."

"Tell me what to do and I'll do it," I replied. "Whatever it takes to put things back how they were, I'll do it. Just tell me how."

Finley's shoulders rolled back. He leaned against the doorway, halfway in, halfway out, while I remained where I'd began, sweating bullets on the stoop.

"We've been friends too long to let something like this get in the way of it," I continued, pressing on. "Come on. Talk to me."

"You hurt my feelings."

"I'm s—"

"Stop apologizing and let me talk."

"S—Alright. Go on."

"You hurt my feelings and I'm upset about it. And that's all. I never said anything about not wanting to be friends."

"I don't know what to say."

"Don't say anything, then."

I closed my eyes and wiped a thick layer of sweat from my forehead. Faint slivers of green stared back at me in the newfound darkness, taunting and jeering like they always did. They were winning our invisible war, and winning it handedly.

"You don't have to do anything," he went on. "Just start acting like you care. I know you're caught up with Kai—"

Laughter burst from my lips. My face burned red as I realized that I had repeated the exact action that had started our fight in the first place. It was instinctual. I couldn't help myself.

"What was that about?"

"Nothing, never mind. Keep going, please."

"No. Tell me what that was."

He shook his head and moved away from the doorframe. A clear pathway into the house presented itself, yet I didn't have the nerve to take it. So I stood still, remaining exactly where I stood.

"I'm serious," he said. "Come inside and tell me what happened. Seriously, I want to know."

Reluctantly, I crossed the threshold and stepped into his house. Most of the lights had been turned off, so we both fumbled foolishly through the darkness until we reached the basement; the TV had been left on down there.

I had no idea if he had forgiven me even partially, but I was in his house and we were talking. That was something in itself. Still, I remained by the door.

"What happened?" he asked, collapsing onto the couch.

"Nothing," I lied.

"Come on." He threw his legs over the arm of the couch and stretched himself out like a fat, tired cat. "You can tell me. Forget about our argument. I'm interested, genuinely."

"Alright, fine," I replied. "But when I'm done, you have to give me the run-down on you and Mathew. It's been forever since we've talked. I've fallen out of the loop."

Finley sat up intently and brought his legs up to his chest. I stayed where I was, but relaxed at the knees as I began to tell him what happened.

"It was all going perfectly," I concluded after outlining our picnic, rock-table and all. "We had just started making out when Tory showed up and everything was ruined."

"I don't think you should let her go," Finley replied. "Not so easily, at least. You need to fight."

"What do you mean?"

"It sounds like she's good for you. And if that's true—if she really is—then you don't have any choice but to fight and keep fighting until you're sure you've lost and it's all over."

"You're probably right, but I don't know what to do."

"Come here," he said, gesturing from me to the spot on the couch next to him and back again. I exhaled slowly, then followed his hand and sat down. He wrapped an arm around my neck and looked me directly in the eyes. "It's simple. Take her advice. Tell her how you feel."

"That's a lot harder—"

"Of course it's going to be hard," he interrupted. "Anything worth doing is. But if you want her back, you have to push through and do it anyway. Explain what happened, all of it, and then find a way to move on, together. It's the only way."

"What if she tells me to go away?"

"Then you apologize again and do what she says. You can't control how she reacts, but you have to try either way. Who knows if you'll get lucky? Maybe she'll forgive you."

"It already happened once today."

He smiled. "Exactly."

Perhaps he was right. An explanation or apology might be enough. Maybe she would understand that I was trying to be better and give me another chance because of it. The entire plan revolved around a whole lot of maybes without a single guarantee to weigh them down, but it was all I had. It was better than nothing, and my only hope. For Kai, that was more than enough to try.

My brain continued to try and process all the possible outcomes as Finley shook my back and tried hyping me up. We were friends again. And if I managed to get Kai back, maybe the summer would be too.

"Why did you do it?" he asked suddenly. My eyes widened. I perked up and looked over at him. "It seemed like you and Kai had a good thing going on. Why risk it for Tory?"

I stared down at the carpet, considering his question. There was no logical explanation for what I'd done. Graduation had shown me her true feelings. She hadn't been vague or subdued at all. She didn't care about me and let the whole school know. Our breakup was a spectacle for all to enjoy. Still, I brought her up to the clearing, but why? Why did I do it?

That simple question pounded into my skull. What made me bring her to Kai's sacred place and risk everything that had graciously fallen into my lap? I had nothing.

"I just missed her, I guess." It was a struggle, articulating the impossible. "Or at least the idea of her. You know, what we could have one day become. It's hard to look back and accept that it was all in my head, that none of it was real."

Finley massaged my neck. "That's not true. You guys just changed over the years, that's all. And your love got twisted somewhere along the way. That doesn't mean it never existed."

"What *does* it mean then?"

"That you weren't meant to be."

"If only I would've realized that before I ruined everything with Kai." I sighed ruefully. "But whatever, there's nothing I can do about it now."

"Don't say that. There's always a way."

"I don't know. How're you and Mathew?"

His eyes fell to the floor just as mine had before. We were both pendulums swinging back and forth, struggling to balance. By deflecting, I pushed my weight onto him so I could swing freely.

"Trouble in paradise?"

He scoffed. "Paradise? That's one way to put it."

"What happened?" I asked. "You guys seemed so good last time we talked. Everything looked perfect."

"That's the problem—nothing has. Everything's exactly the same. We're halfway in and halfway out. Sometimes we're together, sometimes we're not. I can't take it anymore."

I stood up from the couch and began pacing the room, thinking of what I could say that would help him but not overstep our fragilely replastered friendship. "Did you go out?"

"When?"

"After our fight," I replied. "At the beach."

He nodded.

"Is that when you realized nothing was going to change?"

"Pretty much," He sighed. "We hung out all night and acted like we were a couple. But when the sun came up we weren't anymore. It's a breakup every time we say goodbye."

"That's no way to live."

"Not at all. But there's nothing I can do about it."

"You could give him an ultimatum. It's risky, but it's a whole lot better than nothing. You can't keep running forever."

"There's too much at stake, too much to lose."

"Is losing him really worse than what you've got?" I questioned. "Are you okay with this going on indefinitely? Because that's what's going to happen if you don't put a stop to it now. He'll push and push until you finally break."

"But—"

"Think about Bloomington."

"Bloomington's why I can't."

"I don't understand."

"He runs the best house on campus."

"So what? What's that got to do with anything?"

"I don't want to be known as the stupid freshman that had a chance at the best house and blew it because he thought he deserved a label with the president."

"You're not just some freshman, though. It's obvious that he likes you. What grade you're in shouldn't matter."

"But it does."

"Maybe," I conceded. "Still, I think you'd be surprised."

A heavy sigh escaped his lips. The anxiety in the room was palpable. "Be honest. What do you think I should do?"

"Tell him how you feel. See where that takes you."

His body tensed, and his hands clinched into two tight fists. He took a collected breath inward, then exhaled slowly. "I can't do that, no way."

I sat next to him and looped an arm over his shoulder, pulling him flush against me. "Neither can I," I said. "That's why we need each other."

"What do you mean?"

"Doing it together makes sure the other follows through. That way we'll both go to bed with an answer, good or bad."

"Alright," he agreed. "When do we do it?"

"Tomorrow."

"Where?"

"The beach," I replied. "Where else?"

15

Frigid water fell from the showerhead, cascading onto me. My muscles tensed as it slid down and covered my back before falling to the ground and forming a puddle around my feet. Horrible pain came temporarily, but subsided quickly. By the time I'd rinsed the shampoo from my hair, I was wide awake and ready.

I stepped out of the shower and began drying myself off, then tossed the towel aside and thumbed Finley a text. *Leaving soon*, I wrote. *Make sure you're ready.* Once the text had sent, I set my phone down and got dressed before heading outside. Summer was waning and waning fast. The time had come to act.

In my head, the plan I'd concocted was ready for execution. Water still dripped from my hair, staining the back of my leather seat, but I was ready to go. I shifted into reverse, backed out of the driveway, and accelerated toward Finley's house. If all went well, the world would soon be returned to its proper axis.

Most of the roads were empty, which made sense. It was early on a Monday morning. Most of the locals were back at work, and the out-of-towners had returned to their condos in the city. All that remained on the roads were high schoolers and college kids on vacation, but most of them were either too drunk or hungover to be out driving.

Finley's neighborhood felt the same when I pulled up, half asleep, deadly silent. Only a few of the houses had cars in the driveways and their lights turned on inside. His wasn't one of them. When I reached the door I pounded until it swung open.

"What're you doing here?" he asked, yawning from inside the house. I remained on the stoop. "It's not even seven yet."

"I told you yesterday. Let's go."

He propped himself up against the doorframe and yawned again. "What're you talking about?" he asked, very obviously half-asleep. "You didn't tell me anything."

"The *plan*," I replied angrily, pushing past him as I stepped into the house. "Doing it together—remember?"

"Oh, yeah. I didn't realize it'd be this early."

"It's the only way."

He groaned and led me into the kitchen. I leaned against the countertop and watched him put on a pot of coffee. "So what're we going to do?" he asked. "How're we going to win them back?"

"We're going to the beach."

"Great plan," he scoffed, laughing as he pulled two mugs out of the cupboard and sat them next to the hissing coffee pot. "What will that accomplish?"

"If we can get there before them everything just might work out for us. But we have to get there first. Otherwise it's no use."

"I still don't get it."

I laughed and took a drink from my mug. It was stifling hot and burned my lips, but tasted good, and more importantly, heavily caffeinated, so I didn't complain.

"What's the plan?" he asked again.

"To accidentally run into them."

"*Accidentally?*"

I nodded. "See, you do understand."

"And how exactly do you plan on this all working out?"

"It's risky—"

"No, it's stalking."

"Maybe, but it just might work. They go to the beach almost

every day. Both of them, we know this as fact. And if they continue following that same pattern and show up today, we'll be there. We'll be at the clearing, watching. We'll be waiting."

"That's a terrible plan."

"It's the only one we've got."

He took another drink from his mug before turning it upside down and dumping the rest into the sink. "Oh, yeah, there's no way this'll blow up in our faces."

"Have a little faith. It'll seem romantic looking back."

"Whatever you say."

"Nobody's ever regretted taking the leap."

"I don't think that's true," Finley said. He grabbed a hoodie from the back of the door and pulled it over his head. "But I don't have anything better to do, so let's do it, I guess."

Most of the coffee was still in my mug, yet I dumped it all into the sink with a smile on my face. It was finally happening. We were leaving, moving forward. And I was about to get her back.

Finley's front door swung open and smacked the doorframe, continuing to bounce against it as we piled into my car.

It only took fifteen minutes to reach the beach—traffic hadn't picked up yet—but my nerves compounded the brief minutes into long hours that stretched to days and years that felt like forever.

My knuckles were a pale white, wrapped tightly around the steering wheel. I parked in the lot near Stop 4. Finley glanced in my direction. I gave him a nod, then we both got out of the car. Crisp morning air blew across the lake and over the sand dunes, providing a nice contrast to my clammy hands. We walked down to the water and hugged the coastline.

"What if this doesn't work?" Finley asked. He spoke into the breeze, over the roaring waves that drenched our feet. "Maybe we should let it go. Move on with our lives."

"There's a decent chance it won't," I replied. "But there's also a chance it will. You said it yourself last night. Kai might take me back, just like Matthew might want to make things official with you. We won't know until we try. Chance is better than certainty when certainty is guaranteed failure. Don't you think?"

"Ask me again in a few hours."

"Fair enough." I laughed.

"It just feels like we're walking to the electric chair," he elaborated. "After trying and convicting ourselves."

His logic was hard to refute, so I just shook my head until the moment had passed and silence was upon us once more. We walked a few hundred more feet like that, then hooked a sudden right before beginning our final ascent.

Each step brought us closer to the Grove. Our heads were hung low. We climbed fast, panting hard, much too tired and out of shape to worry about how it could go wrong.

The dirt of the Grove felt much cooler than the sun-exposed sand of the dunes. Finley's eyes were filled with apprehension. He'd never been to the clearing before. I gave him what I hoped was an encouraging smile, and told him we were almost there. The finish line was close; we just had to cross it.

Traversing the mangled vegetation that made up the underbelly of the trail proved much more difficult than I had imagined. The various smells and noises of the Grove grew louder and more pungent with each step. Birds, then a twig snapping beneath my weight and silence.

The sun floated much higher in the sky when we stepped out from under the canopy of the Grove. It smiled down on us just like it did every other day, totally unaware of our individual lives, unconcerned with what we were doing. We were all inconsequential, abundantly so.

Finley rushed over to the clearing's jagged, rocky edge and let out an uninhibited gasp that reminded me of myself the first time I'd seen the view. There are few things in life quite as beautiful as Lake Michigan when viewed from Northern Indiana; the Chicago skyline against the pale blue sky, warm sun reflecting off the water. I stood a few steps behind and smiled ruefully before joining him.

It was far too early in the day for the partiers to arrive, so the beach was perfectly empty. Miles and miles of naked coastline.

Too bad we couldn't enjoy it.

"Now we wait."

Finley sighed. "Now we wait."

• • •

Hours blew slowly across the Great Lake, while we sat on the jagged rocks waiting. Time meant nothing in its majesty. Non-existent on the clearing, nothing more than a pointless abstraction. My pores bled with sweat that rolled from my chin and turned the rock I was sitting on a temporary shade of dark gray before evaporating and going light again.

Music filled our ears as the beach became populated with an ever-growing crowd of loud, dancing drunks, but we said nothing to each other. We just kept waiting. The stakes were too high for small talk or chitter chatter. Waiting demanded perfect concentration. I couldn't allow myself to miss her if she came. She was my last chance at salvation.

Finley sighed and pushed himself forward. His legs swung across the edge of the clearing, dangling over the abyss. Back and forth they went. Back and forth, back and forth. Then, with a malignant sigh, he fell back onto the sand and buried his hands in its warm embrace.

He yelped suddenly, ripping his hands up out of the sand before opening his palm and staring into it. "What is this?"

I squinted my eyes in his direction, but couldn't see anything. The sun was shining far too bright. "What's what?"

"Give me your hand."

I did what he said and offered my hand beneath his. Slowly, he uncurled his fingers and turned his palm upside down. Microscopic grains of sand fell between the cracks of his fingers until they were all gone, then he dropped whatever he was holding into my palm.

Looking down, I saw a weathered guitar pick. Thousands of songs must have flowed through it, straight from the hands of some unknown master. My eyes narrowed. I held it up into the sunlight and examined its engravings.

There were two heavily faded letters carved into the plastic of the guitar pick. One was an obvious "B", while the other looked like an "E", but it'd been carved sloppily, and could've easily been an "F" or even a "K" instead. My interest dissipated the longer I stared. Fifteen seconds passed, then I flicked it off the edge of the clearing. The pick made tiny helicopters through the air and tumbled to the ground, forgotten.

Then I began retracing Kai's usual route. It made a lopsided, wandering sort of triangle that connected the parking lot, Elwood Grove, and the main dune of Stop 2 together. Our perch up on the jagged rocks placed us in the perfect spot to watch them all at once while remaining undetected.

After cycling through the triangle several times, I noticed a thick cluster of yelling teenagers passing beneath. Three of them carried a long fold-out table, while the others struggled with a large Bluetooth speaker blaring an incomprehensible song.

"We can't stay up here all day," Finley muttered.

I continued staring over the dunes, and said nothing.

"It's one o'clock, man. I don't think she's coming."

"Maybe you're right," I said. "You probably are, honestly. But it doesn't matter. I can't leave. If she shows up and I'm not here, I'll never get over it. I can't blow it, not again."

"We could always come back tomorrow."

"That type of thinking only leads one place, giving up."

"What if it takes all day?"

"Then it takes all day. I don't care. She's worth the wait."

"Even if she never shows?"

"What's the alternative?"

"Have you thought about how creepy this looks if she doesn't want you back? At that point you're just a stalker."

"You're up here too, you know."

"Yeah, but it was your idea."

"What else can I do?"

"Oh, I don't know—maybe send her a text."

"Already tried that. Three times, actually. No answer."

Finley grunted, shifting his weight. He craned his neck to see around the rocks jutting out from the sand. Only one of us had a choice. We both knew it wasn't me.

"You should go," I said.

"I'm not trying to convince you to give up." He shook his head back and forth vigorously. "I just want to make sure you're seeing the situation from every angle, that you understand all the possible outcomes."

"You're right," I replied. "I know you are. This *is* creepy, but I don't have a choice. It's something I have to do."

"Just think—"

"I can't afford to think right now," I interrupted. "That's the whole point. That's what you don't understand."

"I don't know, man."

"This is my battle, not yours. Go down to the beach and have a good time. Make something of today."

Finley's eyes narrowed. His lips remained tightly pressed together. "I don't know," he said again.

"Think about it. Your situation with Mathew is totally different than mine. You've got nothing to gain, waiting up here with me. The reward is nowhere near the risk. It's simple math."

"But I'm your best friend."

"So what?" I questioned. "The whole point of today was to set things straight, to win their hearts. Waiting here hoping she'll eventually show is the only way for me, but it's not—"

"I can't leave you up here alone."

"You have to. Text him and tell him you're at the beach and want to meet up. See where he's at and go from there."

"What about the plan?"

"Nothing's changed."

Finley sighed and looked away from me, but slowly nodded in the wind and stood up. His back was turned to me—he faced out toward the beach, overlooking it all—but I knew exactly what he was thinking. I was right. He had no other choice. He had to go.

So he did.

I traced his path with squinted eyes from my perch. Several minutes passed, then his head poked out from under the canopy of Elwood Grove as he stepped onto the sand. He glanced up in my direction, but something was off. His phone was held up to his ear and he was pacing, talking to someone. Mathew, I hoped, but it was impossible to be sure.

Slowly, he began ascending the main dune of Stop 2. He turned around every few steps, looked over his shoulder, and doubled back a few feet, talking all the while. Then, suddenly, he pulled the phone from his ear and we locked eyes.

His journey had just begun. Mine remained in limbo.

• • •

Mathew arrived at the beach thirty minutes later. He greeted Finley with a tight hug and a very public kiss, directly on the lips. Four other presumed brothers followed shortly after. They all huddled around Finley and Mathew. Together, they created a loose circle in the sand, laughing and joking as they pulled bottles out of their bags and took heavy swigs from them.

Forgotten up on the clearing, I shifted my weight and retraced Kai's triangle again. The beach had turned into a conveyor belt in the time that had passed since Finley left. Half-baked zombies marched from Stop 2 to the parking lot, replaced by a steady stream of fresh, sober lookalikes.

A thin, wispy-looking silhouette of a girl passed beneath and looked up in what I thought to be my direction. But the sun was shining much too bright for me to see her face clearly. All I knew was that she wasn't alone. There was a short, stout man with her. He threw his arm over her shoulder, following a half-step behind.

Their gait was slow, lethargic. Fifty feet took them the better part of fifteen minutes to traverse. They appeared much more concerned with each other than whatever direction they happened to be headed in. Each step was a journey within itself. Then, standing directly beneath me in my lone blind spot, they stopped. The man looked out toward the water.

The girl looked straight up.

It was Kai.

No amount of introspection or mental preparation could have prepared me for the adrenaline and anxiety that shot through my veins when our eyes met. Thousands of hypothetical scenarios flashed through my mind, each worse than the last, yet they all lead to the same grim conclusion. Reality, the crushing of dreams.

It didn't take long for the man she was with to take notice of her quivering eyes and follow them up to me. We made direct eye contact. He smiled and squeezed her waist, nodding slightly as he whispered something unintelligible into her ear.

Kai giggled momentarily, then shook her head and stepped forward in the direction of the Grove—alone.

I shoved my palms into the rock I'd been sitting on, and thrust myself to my feet. My arms pumped through the air and my lungs exploded as I sprinted back down the trails. Sweat exploded from my pores as I ran.

She stood waiting for me on the other side.

"I—"

"What were you doing up there?" she asked. "I didn't think you'd have the nerve to come back after what happened."

"It's the only place that could work."

"Work? What do you mean?"

"I've been waiting all—"

"Hold on, what did you just say?" she questioned. "Have you been up here stalking me?"

"No, not stalking—*waiting*. There's a difference."

Kai snorted in my face and glanced back toward the man she'd came with. I couldn't see him—a thick crop of trees separated the two of us—yet I knew he was there, just out of sight, lingering. "Of course," she mocked. "There always is with you."

"I need to talk to you, and this is only way I knew how. You wouldn't answer my texts."

"Because there's nothing left for us to talk about."

"Come on, Kai."

"What's done is done."

"Please, just let me explain."

"Explain what?" she retorted. "How your ex-girlfriend showed up right before you were about to finally fuck me? You think you can explain that, Louie? Really?"

"I didn't want her to show up."

"Oh, okay. Well that makes everything okay."

"That's not—"

"No, no," she interrupted. "You're right. You're absolutely right. You didn't do anything wrong. *I'm* the crazy one here. Yes, it's all my fault. You bringing her up there was all my fault."

"It was a mistake bringing her. I know that and so do you. But there's nothing I can do about it now."

She stared at me with cold, vacant eyes.

"You're the only one I want."

"Great job showing it."

"If I could go back in time and take it all back I would—I'd do it in a heartbeat—but I can't. All I can do now is apologize and try to make things right. So that's what this is. I'm sorry."

She shook her head and backed slowly into the trees. "No," she said. "It's too late now. Whatever we had is over."

"I'm sorry," I said again.

Her foot traced slow, methodic circles into the dirt. She stared into the ground and avoided my eyes. "Why'd you do it?" she asked quietly.

A bead of sweat fell from my forehead and stained my glasses, blurring my vision. "Honestly, I have no idea. I think I just missed her, what we used to have."

"That's not good enough."

"I was lonely and insecure and chasing the past when I bumped into her on the beach. It was right after our first fight and—"

"After our fight?" Her voice was hallow.

"I'm not proud of it, but it's the truth."

"Don't be sorry," she said, speaking in tight, curt syllables. "It is what it is. Forget about it. Leave me alone."

My mouth opened, intent on responding, but my lips didn't move. No words came out. Nothing, not even one. I had taken my ex-girlfriend to the one place my kind-of-newish-girlfriend-but-not-really held sacred and lost everything because of it. Kai was walking away, and she would never turn around again. We were over, for good, and there was nothing I could do about it.

I stumbled over to the tree Kai had been leaning against and collapsed at its base. The dirt felt cool, but the sand was hot and burned my legs. I wiped my eyes and inhaled. The air reeked of her perfume. I took another breath and closed my eyes, savoring her essence before it disappeared for good. When I finally broke and exhaled everything was black.

Uncle Andrew's eyes stared back at me in the warm darkness. They were bright and green, and surprisingly, not alone. I was lost in a sea of imaginary people. Misery bubbled a slow boil in the pit of my stomach, demanding to be felt. Nobody would come to my rescue, I knew that for certain. They didn't care enough to save me. Salvation was impossible.

Forget about it, she'd said.

Words forever engrained in my mind, reverberating again and again through the twinkle of his green eyes as he continued to laugh and smile and taunt. His voice was hers, and it was all I could hear. There was no escape, just the truth she'd left me with.

Forget about it. Leave me alone.

16

Finley pranced around his basement a man victorious. Back and forth he went, creating an invisible line of footsteps connecting the TV, door, and stairs. He'd invited me over to watch the NBA play-offs, but his mind was miles away. His feet clamored against the hardwood. Pitter patter, pitter patter, pitter patter they went. I wondered if he even knew who was playing.

Suddenly, he stopped pacing and dove next to me on the couch. He grabbed my shoulders and began telling me all about what happened with Mathew on the dune. I kept quiet throughout his entire story and didn't say a word about Kai and the mysterious other-guy she'd been with.

When he asked me directly if she ever ended up showing up, I muttered quietly that she had before demanding he tell me more.

"We played a few games of beer pong, then snuck away from the other guys and took a walk along the water."

"And?" I encouraged. "What'd you talk about?"

"What we are and where we're going."

"How'd that go?"

"Way better than I thought."

"Did you give him an ultimatum?"

"Didn't have to." He jumped back up from the couch, stood

in front of me, and smiled widely. "He said that being together felt right, and that he wanted to give us dating a try, for real."

I glanced away from his eyes. "That's good," I said. "That's really good. I'm happy for you."

Finley's arms went limp and fell lifeless to his side. He remained in front of me. The tension heightened. It was tangible, almost overwhelming. "What's wrong?"

"Nothing."

"There's obviously something. What is it?"

My chest deflated. I sunk into the couch. "I'm sorry," I replied. "It's not you or him, honestly—it's me."

"What's that supposed to mean?"

"She came," I whispered.

"You said—"

"And we talked."

"How'd that go?"

"So much worse than I imagined."

"What happened?"

"I begged her for another chance. She told me to never talk to her again. And she seemed serious."

Finley sat back down, much closer to me than before. He placed his hand on my leg and left it there. It didn't move an inch. Years of unspoken, unquantifiable emotions came flooding out in the ensuing silence.

My love with Tory had all been a lie. Her world was a collection of binaries, nothing more. Everything had to be right or wrong in order to make sense to her. Good or bad, in love or disposed of. One day I found myself on the wrong side of things and was promptly discarded because of it. And that was us, over.

It all made so much sense as I gazed into Finley's steel blue eyes, but it was too late to matter. Kai was different, but I'd treated her just the same. The roles reversed and our relationship was a lie—was it even a relationship? Could I call it that?

There was so much deception entrenched between the two of us and our "relationship" that I could hardly tell. I'd treated her like a self-help tool without ever realizing it, a subconscious means to an end, the vehicle rather than the destination.

I shoved myself off the couch with a frenetic rush of adrenaline. I'd wasted my life crying about the past and pining my hopes on the hypothetical tomorrow, but no more. Kai was gone and it was all my fault. I had to run to edge of the mountain and jump off into the abyss.

It was time to take the leap. I had to change.

"I'm sorry," I muttered, speaking semi-incoherently. "I'm sorry, but I can't be here right now. I've got to go."

"Wh—" Finley began to say, but the door had slammed shut before he could get it out.

And I was gone, halfway to my car.

17

Sun bled through my bedroom window. It doused my mattress and the hardwood floor with its welcoming light. It all looked so peaceful, I thought. Beautiful, the exact opposite of how I felt. Sighing, I rolled off the bed, got on my hands and knees, and began searching for my laptop.

I hadn't written a single word in months, so it was rather hard to find. In the time that had elapsed, the laptop had somehow managed to work itself into the corner where my two walls intersected and lodged itself there. A grunt escaped from my mouth as I hyperextended to reach it.

When I finally managed to wrap my fingers around its dusty edge and pull the laptop out, I sat on the edge of the bed and rested it on my knees.

I opened the screen and gave the power button a try. Fans hummed softly against the exposed skin of my legs. A pale blue light flashed across the cracked screen. It worked.

My hips rotated back, crashing into the headboard as I swung my legs onto the bed. The laptop's screen flickered off with even the most subdued of movements, but always came back quickly. I adjusted my weight; it cut out again. An exhausted pair of eyes stared back at me. Another sigh. Fingers dancing across the keys, constructing a story I thought I'd never willfully tell.

Remaining focused was a constant struggle. I had no choice but to see it out until the bitter end. The alternative would be giving up. So I shook my head and I closed my eyes.

His eyes, big and green and menacing, were there just like they always were. But this time I ground my teeth together and stared back into them willingly. I knew they wouldn't be leaving, and that they probably never would. One thing had changed, however. Neither would I.

The first few sentences came easy, but then I hit a brick wall and my brain froze. My fingers stalled, lingering on the touchpad. A blank white Word document stared back at me. My cursor blinked. There was an infinite number of possibilities, yet not a single road traveled. No assurances, no certainties.

My eyes squinted forward in concentration. My thumbs rubbed the edges of the touchpad. I wanted nothing more than to leap forward and burst through the wall I'd spent thirteen years carefully constructing, but my brain and fingers refused. They stagnated, refusing to sync. I had nothing.

I continued to stare, frozen with my mind concentrated solely on two things: Kai, and Uncle Andrew. Two green eyes piercing through her impossible beauty; everything wrong coupled with everything right. Only one could win.

Articulating how I felt with words proved next to impossible, but it was my only chance. Even if I failed miserably, it would still be worth it. It had to be. Kai told me so. I tensed my hands and forced my fingers to go:

I was five years old when my life changed forever. A typical day that left me irreparably broken. My childhood dead, innocence gone. One night was all it had taken to reduce my existence to a meaningless nothing floating aimlessly for thirteen years, lost in the gap of boyhood and man.

Prior to that day, I only wanted one thing: to be grown up. I had looked all around me and saw grown-ups strong and able to stand up for themselves. They got what they wanted and I couldn't. I was worse than weak, less than zero. All I did was cry. I refused to fight.

He won effortlessly, and I was forever crippled because of it. Or at least that's what I thought. Many of the effects remain today, but not all of them. Sure, I still see his green eyes whenever I close my own, and I hear his taunting voice serenading victory. And they'll probably never go away. He's always there, he's always watching, but he doesn't have control.

Not anymore. I'm taking it back.

My words, though sloppy and unedited, flowed quickly. Once the seal had been broken, the tap ran free. Salty tears blossomed from the corners of my eyes and slid down my cheeks, falling onto the back of my hands as they forced out the vulnerable words.

Then they froze. My eyes snapped shut. The bedroom turned to a treadmill. I couldn't get off. It was moving too fast. I was running forward as quickly as I could. Where I was headed, I had no idea, just that I had to go—fast.

It was my first sleepover, and he was my uncle. But it didn't matter at the time. None of it did. He was godless and amoral and I was desperate to be a man, the perfect storm. I was staying at a house that wasn't my own and blinded by the excitement of it all.

Everything started off so well when I first arrived. It was exactly what I'd expected and so much more. We all shared an early lunch together. Mom was tired and stressed out from work, and so was he. But they all pulled it together and we laughed from the pits of our stomachs as we discussed the upcoming school year, kindergarten, and what it would be like.

When the levy of tears broke it broke truly. They tumbled down from my eyes and coated the backs of my hands as they typed, stopping me dead in my tracks. The gravitas of the moment was far too much. Every word was a dogfight. Each compounded with the last and made the one after even more difficult to force out. I was losing, but I was trying. I was moving forward.

• • •

By the time I was able to collect myself and tab the indent button, writing was synonymous with war. Insecurity waged against my newfound desire for truth. Coupled with the fear, I was immobilized. Whatever choice I made next would dictate the rest of my life. Good or bad, right or wrong. It was my last chance to finally break free from his shackles and live a life of my own.

I remember Mom crying before she left. Her tear-stained face staring down on me in his driveway is a memory I won't soon forget. She told me over and over again that we could call it off and try again some other time, but I wouldn't hear it. "Maybe next week?" she asked hopefully before getting into her car.

But I said no, and told her she was just worried and being way too overprotective. The irony's almost funny, looking back. She had provided me with the perfect out and I'd rejected it gleefully, with a smile on my face. There's nothing quite like the confidence and naivety of a child-aged fool. I was willing to do whatever it took to prove that I was a grown man.

Turns out it took everything.

But I didn't know that back then. Uncle Andrew smiled and reassured us both, then Mom got into her car and that was that. My fate was sealed. Seeing her waning headlights in the driveway was a welcome sight. It was the most beautiful thing I'd ever seen.

A new beginning, I was sure of it.

Come nightfall, I would've done anything for them to return.

I shoved the laptop off my knees. The tears continued falling, painting the sheets around me dark. Watching my deepest insecurities spill from my brain into the world felt real in a way that I never could have imagined.

Yet my fingers kept twitching. They were revving to go, urging me onward. Keep going, they pled. Keep going, keep going, keep pushing. Keep writing until you can't write anymore.

There wasn't any other choice, really. The article wasn't a masturbatory act, but rather one of community, of solidarity and togetherness. There were faceless variants of myself scattered across the globe. From Jakarta to Istanbul, it didn't matter. They all deserved a voice, and I was going to give it to them no matter what it took. I put my head down and began typing once more:

But they didn't. Her headlights never came back. Mom was nowhere to be found. I'd gotten everything I wanted and hated it. She wasn't coming back. I was too young to fend for myself but it was the only choice I had. She wasn't coming back.

I was alone. Completely alone.

There wasn't anywhere to hide or anyone to turn to when our perfect one-on-one sleepover went south, when the lights turned off and the monster came out. I had just started to drift away and fall asleep when he stumbled over to my makeshift bed on the couch.

At first, I didn't think much of it. Heavy footsteps were to be expected. I thought he probably was just going to the bathroom.

Things began to shift when I felt the soft fabric of his sweatpants brushing against my left arm, but not entirely. I still smiled when I sat up.

If only I knew what would come next.

I slammed the laptop shut, sat up, and looked myself over in the mirror at the foot of my bed. My cheeks were blood red, hair matted from hours of anxious sweat. I looked terrible—even that was an understatement—but I had taken the first step.

It was still in the most infantile of forms, but the article had been birthed. I was writing, finally moving forward instead of back, taking action. My days of running were over. I refused to hide from the backs of my own eyelids.

If he stared, I would stare right back.

18

Two scenarios dangled in front of me as I roared down the highway. One of them made perfect sense; it was the obvious, logical choice, while the other begged and tugged at my heartstrings. Turn around, the rationale choice pled. Just head home. But the other was much louder, and much more enticing.

Go to her, get her back—run!

My fingers gripped the wheel tight as my foot pushed down on the gas pedal. I accelerated through a freshly turned red light, contemplating the article as I did.

Northwestern wouldn't give me what I wanted. It couldn't, and neither could any girl. Her greatness was irrelevant. Kai had known this the entire time, of course. That's why she told me to start writing. It was the only thing that could set me free, because it came from me, myself. There were no external factors. My story was my greatest gift. It always had been.

Speeding down the highway, I began to internally rationalize that my newfound perspective was evidence that I'd changed, that because of it our fledgling romance deserved one more chance.

Starting at graduation, my life had been systematically atomized and stripped until nothing remained, leaving me raw and deeply exposed. My internal composition had been fundamentally changed. I'd started writing, and through that, I'd finally began to take back control. The future wasn't mine. It was ours.

My hands were dripping with clammy sweat by the time I turned into Kai's cul-de-sac. I blinked hard. A few tears fell, but not nearly as much as before. Still, I wiped them away. It was crucial that I focused solely on the mission ahead. Chance and spontaneity had brought us together once. I feared I wouldn't get so lucky the second time around.

The streets were mostly empty. Her neighborhood was quiet as I rolled to a stop near the end of her driveway. I shifted my car into park and opened the door before I could talk myself out of turning around. I didn't even bother turning the car off. Either way, it'd only be a short idle.

Anxiety permeated just beneath the surface of my skin in the walkup to her front door. It compounded with each step, doubling as it folded into itself. I balled my hand into a tightly wound fist, brought it up to the wood, and began to knock—one, two, three. Salty sweat droplets fell from my eyebrow, staining the concrete of the stoop below. The door swung open. Time stood still.

But it wasn't Kai standing on the other side. No, it was the other-guy, from the beach.

"Who are you?" His voice was deep and raspy and sounded much more masculine than mine. "What are you doing here?"

I took a half-step back, but remained firmly on the stoop. "I'm looking for Kai," I said. "Is she home?"

He grunted, sizing me up and down.

"Can I talk to her?"

"Who are you?" he asked again.

"My name's Louie. Can I talk to her now?"

"Louie," he said slowly. "Never heard of you before. What do you need to talk to her about?"

"None of your business. It's private."

He laughed and shook his head. My cheeks burned red with insecurity. "Whatever. I'll go tell her some random guy showed up. She can come down if she wants. I don't care."

The door slammed in my face.

I had no idea who the other-guy was, but I was sure that I hated him. He acted so pompous, referring to me as "some random guy" when I meant so much more to her than he ever would. Eventually, we would end up back together and he would understand that he lost and I won. But until then he held all the power. I was stuck on the outside looking in, out on the literal stoop.

I stepped forward and pressed my ear against the door. There were faint, receding footsteps just out of reach on the other side. I tried straining myself to hear better, but it was no use. My foot tapped up and down on the concrete as my insides writhed inward at the thought of how Kai would react to the other-guy's descripttion of me. There was no way it would be flattering.

Naturally, he would present me in the most unflattering way possible, describing in great detail the meekness of my composition, the foul-smelling desperation exuding from my pores, how fidgety I was speaking to him. I just hoped that he would say my name and she saw through everything else.

The footsteps picked up in volume. They sounded much closer than before. Tap tap, tap tap, tap tap—they stopped, and it was silent for a moment. Then came a flutter of unintelligible whispering, undercut by a deep, masculine belly laugh. The door nearly knocked me off the stoop when it swung open.

Kai stood on the other side, staring at me.

"What are you doing here?" she asked in a low voice that hit hard in the gut. "Didn't I make myself clear at the beach?"

"You did, but this is dif—"

"No it's not," she interrupted. "This isn't different at all. You had a second chance and you blew it. Now give up. Move on."

"I can't. We need to talk."

"First you stalk me at the beach, now you show up at my house unannounced. What's next? Where does this end?"

"I know it looks terrible," I conceded. "But everything's different now. I've changed. I'm better."

She scoffed. "Impossible. Nobody changes this fast."

"Let me prove it to you. Please, I'm begging."

"No," was all she said at first. Then she shook her head and leaned up against the doorframe, repositioning herself so that she stood between the other-guy and me. "It's over. There's nothing left for you to prove."

"You don't understand."

"No. I don't care."

Mouth slightly ajar, I looked at her desperately but couldn't find the words to say. My lips wouldn't move. Nothing would be enough. I was hopeless.

"Even if you have changed," Kai continued, "it doesn't matter. I've already made my decision. There's no going back."

"But—"

"I'm sure you'll be great one day. But unfortunately, that day's not today. You've let me down enough for a lifetime."

The article had changed me, but it hadn't us.

"I think you should go," she whispered.

The other-guy from the beach snickered, still hidden by the door, and I trudged back to my car. Head hanging low, I got inside. It took three attempts to fit my keys into the ignition and start the engine. Kai's house shrunk slowly in my rearview mirror before finally succumbing to the horizon. The shame remained.

• • •

My house was empty when I got home. I turned my car off and trembled in the newfound silence without moving, contemplating the article waiting for me under my bed. Exhaling deep through my sternum, I got out and rushed inside.

Seconds after stepping into my bedroom, I fell to my knees and began digging for the laptop again. Locating it proved much easier the second time around. I pulled it out and jumped onto the bed. It creaked under my weight, moaning as I rotated my hips and pushed them back into the headboard. I tabbed the next indent after staring blankly at the screen a while.

For years, I thought what happened to me meant that I was gay. My juvenile brain told me that was simply how the world worked, that something about me attracted him and what happened that night was inevitable. It was all my fault, somehow.

I caused it.

Looking back, of course, I realize that my logic wasn't sound. But it was more than enough to have childhood-Louie convinced he was gay, and he wouldn't hear a word otherwise. Everything was so simple, perfectly straight, yet incongruent and terrible.

There was one critical flaw in my newfound knowledge, however: I wasn't attracted to other boys whatsoever. I felt nothing when I looked at the boys in my class or on TV or anywhere else. No, I always felt myself drawn to the girls. But that couldn't be.

I had to be gay.

So where did that leave me? How would I ever make it in the world if I couldn't even get being gay right?

I had only written two paragraphs, yet my eyes were already damp with the pain of thirteen years suppression. I glanced up and began rereading my words. It was far too early to tell if they were good or not, but they were undeniably true and that was enough. I had to keep going. I had to force my story out.

I questioned myself every day growing up. No matter what I tried, the math just wouldn't add up. Many years passed before I began to realize the critical flaw in my childhood logic. One false conclusion dictated the course of my life for well over a decade.

I was the gay kid who wasn't gay. The kid who got molested by his uncle and couldn't figure out what that meant. My head was foggy, terribly so. And I couldn't see a thing.

It didn't help that he was always around. Every birthday party, vacation, Thursday evening dinner—he was there, taunting me. I couldn't tell if it was just my brain playing tricks on me, but it always felt like he was openly mocking me with his smirks and smiles and subtle double entendres at the dinner table.

Throughout it all, he consistently acted like nothing had happened between the two of us. It was so convincing that nobody ever would have believed me if I told them.

He was a good man with a good reputation, a man who would never, ever do something so heinous. His act nearly had me convinced at times. So I kept my mouth shut. I told no one.

I took his piercing green eyes in stride. I stumbled through the terror of each blink and sleepless night for years by myself in hopes that one day they would eventually go away.

But they didn't, and deep down I knew that they never would. Not unless I stood up, unless I demanded to be counted.

The laptop screen had gotten progressively blurrier the longer I typed. Tears accumulated, and despite wiping them away, it was a struggle to see. My brain began to wander, and I asked myself uncomfortable questions without obvious answers.

What would I do with the article once it was finished? Who would dare publish it? And afterward, what would my life become? How would the people in my life react? Would my darkest childhood fear come to life, or would they accept me and love me regardless? Would they even believe me?

The only way that I would ever be able to find the answers to any of my questions was if I continued to write and kept going until the universe was forced into playing its hand. Passivity would always fail. The muscles in my hands tensed as I prodded internally at the beat of my story. They danced solemnly across the keyboard and returned to work.

I think that a part of me has always known that this would be how things ended between the two of us—war. One of us would inevitably take a stand and the entirety of our shared past would be dredged out. Then the court of public opinion would have its say, and a winner would emerge victorious. The loser would be forever exiled.

The only problem was that his story was masterfully concocted and perfectly planned, while mine was not. He'd spent a lifetime constructing an undetectable alter ego, force-feeding his lies to all of Long Beach. Our family, the school—nobody was safe. So I conceded and succumbed to silence.

But not anymore. Everything's different now.

It all changed when I met a girl. Earlier this summer, at the beach when I least expected it, I stumbled upon her. She asked me what I wanted out of life, and when I told her I wanted to be a writer she said that I needed to write, that was all.

In her eyes, credibility and degrees were nothing more than expensive wall decorations. They didn't matter. Nothing did but my story, the truth. Most importantly, she didn't run when I told her mine.

She didn't laugh or treat me any differently, either. No, nothing changed at all, and my faith in humanity was restored because of it. The world wasn't so bad, after all. It's just a collection of semi-connected people leading incongruent lives doing the best they can.

When we die, our lives are nothing more than a series of facts preserved or forgotten. Here are mine:

1. *My name is Louie Benet.*
2. *I was molested by my Uncle Andrew when I was five years old.*
3. *I'm not a victim.*
4. *He doesn't control me.*

Believe them or don't. Either way, it won't change anything, least of all the truth. Nothing will. I am what I am and what I'm always going to be. My fate was sealed long ago. Your acceptance of me and my story is irrel-evant, as is theirs.

And, just like that, the article was finished. I pressed down on the "enter" key twice, then tabbed the mouse until my cursor blinked in the center of the page. ***THE END***, I typed in big, bold letters. My fingers trembled more than they ever had before.

The article wasn't polished whatsoever—it was several drafts away from being presentable—but it was done and that meant everything. My words had broken free from the prison of my mind.

Finally, they'd been released into the real world. A rueful

smile rolled over my face. My story was out.
There was no turning back.

19

Three days had passed since I'd finished the article. Much of that time was spent refining the first draft. Chopping up the prose, rewriting parts, and reshaping it all to make it presentable. This process repeated itself until my story was out of my brain and onto the page in a way that I could be proud of.

After sitting on the completed draft a while, I began scouring the internet for the email addresses of anyone I thought could be even remotely useful for securing some kind of distribution. Traditional presses, alternative pubs, microscopic blogs—I tried them all. Going wide indiscriminately gave me the best possible chance of something eventually sticking, I thought. Just one yes, that was all I needed for everything to change.

Yet all my emails fell upon dead eyes. Not a single person I reached out to bothered getting back to me. It was like they didn't care, like my story was irrelevant. Still, my spirits remained high.

I cruised down the highway with the windows down, reveling in the cool, Wednesday evening breeze a changed man. Birds chirped, leaves rustled, and I continued to ride. Nobody had shown any interest, but I would find a way. That much I was sure of, even if I had to do it all myself.

Somehow, someway, our story would be heard.

Accelerating toward the Peter Cat, I began to consider Mom's reaction to the article. My heart sank. It went even deeper when I thought about Finley and his. Would they take my side? I wondered. Would they believe me?

No matter how they reacted, I knew their worlds would be irreversibly changed. Good or bad, their grip on reality would be forever altered. People tend to behave erratically when that's the case. I drove on. There was nothing else I could do.

My first glimpse of the Peter Cat was the old man. As I drove past the back of the building, I saw him outside smoking by the garage. He stared wistfully into the air with every puff. I pushed down on the horn twice in quick succession and gave him a light, jolting startle. He threw an arm up into the air, cigarette bouncing against his bottom lip. I parked in the spot closest to the door and nearly ran inside.

"*Ça va?*" the old man exclaimed as I stepped into the cafe. He had just come inside himself, and was getting situated behind the espresso machine. The entire place reeked of old cigarettes.

"It's been one hell of a summer."

Never a man of many words—or a particularly big fan of the English language—the old man simply grunted unintelligibly before asking what I wanted to drink.

"Tea sounds good."

"*Au lait?*" he asked.

"Extra, please."

He nodded, then began filling a tea pot with water. Once he'd finished, he placed it on the stove behind him and turned the burner all the way up. The old man was obsessed with preparing the drinks by hand. When he was working, he viewed the Peter Cat as an extension of his personal home back in Lyon. Paying customers were indistinguishable from lifelong friends in his eyes.

After ordering my drink, I returned to my usual booth by the window and sat down. A small, leatherbound paperback sat next to me, nestled halfway into the old cushion. I pulled the book out and worked my fingers over its spine.

It was heavily cracked and dry, rough to the touch. *Le Mort*, read the cover, a title I didn't recognize. I thumbed through the pages to investigate further, but it was all in French, so I tossed the book aside and looked out the window instead. Things were much simpler that way.

Dark stains blotted the white paint of the sills. Years of bugs and condensation compounded and proved impossible to clean, far too powerful for whatever chemicals they had on hand. It was disgusting to look at, yet somehow beautiful too.

They connected all of Long Beach, the blotted stains. Countless people had been exactly where I was, sitting in the exact same booth doing the exact same thing. They set their coffees and teas on the windowsill and watched the people passing by, presumably lost in thought just like I was. A young Korean man walked past with a crestfallen face and an armful of cherry blossoms, most of which were dead. And those that weren't soon would be.

I diverted my eyes from the window. They eventually settled back on the old man. I studied him as he worked, as he pulled the pan of boiling water from the stove and poured it into to a porcelain mug, then grabbed two tea bags—one would never do—and tossed them in. Finally, he dumped a heavy-handed shot of milk into the mug and finished it off with a drizzle of fresh honey.

My brain came to a slow, yet sudden realization as he finished my cup. I was witnessing the old man fulfill his life's great purpose in real-time. The vast majority of people just float through life reacting to whatever's going on around them, but not him. The old man knew exactly what he wanted and chased after it until it happened. He traveled from the outer banlieues of Lyon to a modest cafe just south of Chicago.

Neither of us had a choice.

We were exactly the same, slaves to a dream. He served mediocre teas and coffee so he could push great unknown works in a county that was not his own.

I had a story burning inside me, a story thirteen years in the making, a story the world needed to hear. A story only I could tell.

A smile drifted across my face as the old man approached. He had no idea what was going on, but that was the point. He didn't have to. Finally, I could stand on my own.

"*Thé au lait*," he muttered, reaching across the table to place the mug on the stain-blotted windowsill, just like he did every time, just like he did with everybody else.

I looked up, still smiling, and thanked him for all that he'd done for me. His eyebrows furrowed, but he nodded and walked away. The curtains had closed on my part of the story.

What remained was theirs.

20

Two knocks were all it took for Finley's door to swing open. Once it did, he stood on the other side wearing bright pink shorts and looking terribly confused. His shirt was mostly undone, chest exposed. He looked me up and down, yawning. "What are you doing here?"

I glanced over my shoulder. We were completely alone. Yet still, I remained on edge, terrified that someone was near, that they were just out of sight, listening. "Can I come inside?"

He stepped aside. "What's up?"

"There's something I need to tell you."

"Are you okay?"

"Yeah. It's nothing like that. I'm fine."

Finley's shirt lagged behind as he led me through the house into the kitchen. "If it's not that, then what is it?"

I sat down at the breakfast table and sighed. Finley glanced over at me, forehead creased, and put on a fresh pot of coffee. "Are we alone?" I asked. "Is your mom here somewhere?"

The coffee maker whistled as it ground the beans. "What's going on?" Finley asked. He pulled two mugs out of the cupboard and placed them on the counter. "Why're you acting so weird?"

"Just answer the question."

"Alright. We're alone."

I looked around one more time, just to be sure.

"What's going on?" he asked again.

My eyes fell to the floor. At first, I said nothing, studying the grout between the tiles. The coffee maker hissed. Tension filled the room. I sighed. "I wrote something the other day."

Finley grabbed the pot and turned it upside down. Both our mugs filled slowly with its brown, steaming liquid. Its smell lathered the kitchen.

"What am I supposed to do with that information?"

I stared at the floor.

He handed me one of the mugs. I took it and blew over the piping hot coffee. Steam fogged my glasses. "At least tell me what it's about."

Regret constricted around my stomach. I should've stayed at the Peter Cat. "Never mind. It's hard to explain."

"Absolutely not," he replied. "We're not doing that."

"Sorry, bu—"

"No buts. Tell me what it's about."

"You'd have to read it for yourself to understand."

"Alright, then let me read it."

My fingers clinched into a fist beneath the table. Finley had no idea the internal struggle I was enduring. "Fine," I said reluctantly. "What's your email address? I'll send you it."

"You didn't bring it with you?"

I shook my head.

"Why'd you come over?"

My stomach clinched tighter. "To warn you."

"Warn me about what?"

"It'll all make sense once you read it."

• • •

I role-played what I would say to Mom the entire way home. But when I pulled into the driveway, I had nothing. My mind was empty, blank. I stepped out of my car anyway. I'd already told Finley. It was the only way.

When I ran into her in the living room she asked me how my day was. I said nothing. My lips remained tightly pressed against each other. She kept pressing, so I lied and told her that I was just tired and ready for bed.

I didn't sleep, not a wink.

The lights were off; everything was dark. The last few struggling rays of daylight were long gone. I tossed my bag onto the bed and pulled my laptop out, cracking it open to rest atop my outstretched legs.

Pale blue light flickered from the screen, bouncing off my glasses, distorting my reflection. I closed my eyes. All was green. I lived in that space for a while, staring back. When I opened them again, I typed Finley's email address into a blank message, attached the article, and clicked send. The only person I had left to tell was mere feet away, right on the other side of my wall.

Whatever fate destined her reaction to be, I would take it and accept its truth. If her world was to be irreparably broken and stomped to shreds, then she deserved to hear it straight from the source. I owed her that much, at least.

I pushed myself off the bed and began the death march to her bedroom. Each step brought a darker thought, questions without answers. What if she didn't believe me? What if she couldn't cope with the truth? Or worse yet, what if she took his side?

The hallway was even darker than my bedroom. All the light came from the crack under her door. I could hardly see the backs of my own hands, but I kept walking until I reached her door. When I did, I stopped and stood perfectly still. The muffled sounds of late-night TV seeped through. My brain begged me to double back, to reconsider.

I balled my hand into a trembling fist and knocked three times on the door. "Come in!" Mom yelled without hesitation.

My eyes fell to the dimly lit spot between my feet. Her voice faded to nothing. Everything went quiet. Countless what-ifs ran through my head. I was certain I'd made the wrong decision. But there was no going back. It was too late.

"Come in!" she repeated.

I pushed open the door. Light flooded the hallway as I stepped inside. My eyes were fixated on the floor, studying my feet.

"What's going on?" she asked

"Promise me you won't overreact."

"What—"

"Promise me."

"Alright, *fine*. I promise."

Head hung low, I walked to the edge of her bed. All I could see were feet, four of them.

"What's going on?"

My eyes remained exactly where they were. "There's something I haven't told you," I whispered.

"Oh, okay. What is it?"

Her eyes burned into the side of my skull. I shook with anticipation. "It'd be easier if I just showed you."

Mom reached out a hand and guided me to the bed. When I sat down, she rested it atop my knee and left it there, rubbing small circles into it. "Showed me what?"

"It's on my laptop. I'll go get it."

"Why don't you just tell me?" she asked. "You're already sitting here. Might as well just get it out now."

My body tightened into itself. I shook my head and ignored her. She just didn't understand. She wouldn't be able to, not until she read it. I pushed my palms into the mattress and stood up. Her eyes followed me out the door, but I didn't say a word and I kept moving forward.

Forward, forward, forward.

It's the only way.

The lights remained off when I stepped back into my bedroom and grabbed the laptop. I didn't need them to see. Its layout had long been engrained in my mind. The bed tucked beneath the window, the TV directly to the right, resting on a broken, lopsided stand. It was all there, perfectly visible in the abject darkness.

I ran my fingers over the laptop's plastic case and thought one last time about what I was about to do. Thirteen years had beaten me over the head with-out so much as a whimper in protest, then one day, a random girl stumbled into my life at the beach and nothing was ever the same again. Kai had started me down the path, but I was walking it alone.

She told me, in no uncertain terms, that thinking and dreaming were nothing more than worthless verbs without action put behind them. And she was right, all the way down. A person's life is nothing more than a hard-boil of their cumulative actions.

When you die, the good of your life is subtracted from the bad and you're judged on what remains. My life, the article—they were my story, how I would be remembered. That alone made everything worth it, even if she'd never know.

I tucked the laptop under my arm and hurried back into the hallway, then her bedroom. "Here you go," I muttered, dropping it onto her lap before quickly circling back. "Come talk to me when you're finished."

"What is it?" she asked as I walked away.

"Everything. You just have to read it."

21

My knees pressed tightly into my chest. I wrapped my arms around them. Trembling in the fetal position, I was a child for a second time. Only a thin strip of drywall separated me from Mom. Everything was silent.

Just on the other side of the wall, she was reading my article, discovering my secret life, my hidden self. Whatever conclusions she came to, I feared they would be permanent, hard-baked into her perception of me.

The optimistic portion of my brain tried desperately to convince the nihilistic part that she would carefully consider the facts and react rationally to them. My gut remained doubtful. She loved us both. That much was undeniably true. So how would she react when the time came to choose?

Picking me would mean rejecting herself, or at least the reality she'd created and lived within. Uncle Andrew had done the unthinkable to her only child, while she had loved him the entire time and repeatedly let him into our home.

That would be the hardest part, acceptance. She *had* been there the entire time. She did continually invite him over, and she had consistently overlooked the red flags and warning signs. But she also had no idea what he'd done to me. Two things could be true at once without being directly related.

The truth is what the truth was, nothing more.

Once she understood that, both of us could move on, together. The future was all that remained. All I could control was what I did next.

The article was done. Now how would I react? The past would remain the same regardless.

Thirteen years had been reduced to one moment that would dictate the outcome of the rest of my life. All roads would soon converge, the dust would settle, and whatever remained would become the truth. A cluster of tears rolled off my cheek and stained my bedsheet. I sat up.

None of it mattered. Everything did.

Mom's shadow stood in the doorframe. Crickets sung outside my window. The furnace roared from the basement. Tension rose. My fingers shook to the beat of a pulsating brain. We stared, neither of us daring to look into the other's eyes.

"Why didn't you tell me?" she whispered.

I couldn't respond. I couldn't speak.

She took three slow, deliberate steps forward, then placed her palms on either side of my shoulders. "Why didn't you tell me?" she asked again. "Why didn't you ever say anything? I could have done something. I could have stopped him."

Holding my eyes up to meet Mom's gaze was a horrible struggle. Salty tears fought to break free. My skull pounded. "I couldn't find the right words. The moment never came."

"I'm so sorry." Her voice was a whisper. She sat on the edge of my bed and rubbed my kneecap. "You shouldn't have had to go through that alone. I can't believe this. It's all my—"

"No," I interrupted. "It's not."

"But I'm your mother. Keeping you safe is my job."

My eyes fell to the floor, to a carpet I'd stared at thousands of times, a carpet that had absorbed my tears for thirteen long years. I blinked, sighing heartily, but held them in. Mom's fingers traced circles around my kneecap. I flexed instinctually. She sobbed and adjusted her weight. The bedsprings creaked, filling the room. I wrapped my arm around her and held tight.

Suddenly, I was the one comforting her.

"I don't understand. How could Andrew do something like this? After everything we've been through together, after all these years. How could he do it?"

I reached over, grabbed her hand, and gave it a firm, concentrated squeeze. "I've been asking myself the same question for the last thirteen years."

"What'd you come up with?"

"Nothing at all," I replied. "People like him don't need a reason to do what he did. They're sick and twisted. They do whatever they want, hurting people until they die or somebody finally catches on and stops them."

"He's always seemed so normal," she whispered. Her voice was hardly audible, weak and desperate.

"What happened wasn't an accident. No, he'd been planning it for years. And he's good at what he does. Very good, one of the best. Lying comes naturally to him."

Mom's lips trembled. Her eyes slowly rose to meet mine. They were full of tears. "What do we do now?" she asked. "Where do we go from here?"

I looked back at her, but said nothing.

"Am I supposed to confront him?" she continued. "Or should I call the police an—"

"No, no," I interrupted feverishly. "You can't do that. Absolutely not. There's no way."

"What are we supposed to do, then? We can't just let him get away with what he's done."

My hand returned to her kneecap. I gripped it hard. Our eyes locked, lips quivering in perfect unison. Years of unspoken confessionals screamed into the dimly lit bedroom, yet not a single word was spoken.

I had thrust a lifetime of burdens onto her back and asked her to deal with it in real-time. I sighed. "He already has."

She stared back at me, defeated, then slowly nodded her head as the room descended deeper into silence. There would be no justice for me.

The police wouldn't come crashing through the front door. They wouldn't arrest him. They wouldn't save the day.

He got away with it.

"Why now?" Mom asked quietly, breaking the silence. "If you think he's already gotten away with it, why bother writing the article? What's the point?"

"The article's not for me."

"Who's it for?"

"Future versions of me," I replied. "The lost boys to come. Nobody deserves to feel how I did. Like a freak—an outcast. If my story reaches just one of them it'll be worth it."

"Future versions of you?"

"There will always be more."

Her stomach collapsed against my side. She heaved before trembling. Sobs followed shortly after, and her fingers pushed into mine, separating them. Our palms touched. I squeezed.

"What's your plan?" she asked.

"I've already sent it out to a bunch of publications. Major outlets like *The New Yorker* and the *Tribune*, but little places too. I went as wide as I could. If they had a place for submissions or an email address somewhere on their website, I sent them a copy. Now I just need a yes. Just one yes."

"And if you don't get one?" she asked. "What will you do if none of them agree to publish it?"

"Then I'll just keep trying. I'll go back to my laptop, revise the article, rewrite the bad parts, then send it back out for another round until somebody breaks and gives me the yes I need."

"You've got this all figured out, don't you?"

"Not at all," I replied. "But it's necessary. Somebody has to take a stand and do it. Why not me?"

"I would be so scared," she whispered, hand lingering on my knee cap. "What if people don't react how you want them to?"

Her hand traced its way from my knee to my back. The way she rubbed told me everything I needed to know. She believed me. We would be alright.

"It's not ideal, but what other choice do I have? I'm tired of running and hiding and wasting the best years of my life feeling sorry for myself. I refuse to keep going like this. It ends now."

Mom's hand slowed to a stop. Her fingers lingered on my back, perfectly still and comforting. I closed my eyes. The green was gone.

After thirteen long years, the green was gone, replaced by the soft, innocent orange of childhood lost. All the sleepless nights spent crying, blaming myself. It all felt so foolish.

I had pinned all my hopes on the bright lights of the big city, on a J-school that didn't matter. And to support the fiction, I had spun a web of lies propped up by pseudo-rationale so complex that I almost never escaped. But it was all a lie, from top to bottom. Kai made that abundantly clear.

Her influence on me cut so much deeper than any words I would ever write. She carved herself into the very essence of my being. She made me open my eyes and realize that the key to the lock had always been in my hands.

She led me to the answer of my life's greatest question, yet nobody would ever ask about her or know her name, not even my own mother. She would only exist between the lines, forever unspoken, unknown. Exactly what I needed.

I opened my eyes, then closed them again.

Black and only black. My fate, the future. It had always been mine. Her words rang truer than ever before.

Just do the work and they'll find you.

Acknowledgements

I am forever indebted to the following people:

Bobby Lee, for making vulnerable, honest art. Your work inspired me to tell my story and stop hiding from the world. Without you, this book would have forever remained inside.

Scott Semegran, for answering my questions and sharing so much invaluable information. Without you, I would've spent many more months struggling and trying to figure this all out.

And last, but certainly not least, Nick Cole and Hugh Howey for showing the world what independent publishing could truly be.

Even though none of us have ever met, you all have impacted my life in ways I could never articulate. Thank you.

—Nicholas Coursel

About the Author

Nicholas Coursel is a Chicago writer and freelance journalist. His work aims to shed light on the forgotten and embraces his working-class roots. Nicholas has previously published several short stories and select poems. *Just One Yes* is his debut novel.